2038

The New Serenity

Preface

Today, in the year 2038, we have mastered the great crises. It was close, but we made it. The global ecological, social and economic disasters of the 2020s brought people, states, institutions and companies together. They committed themselves to fundamental rights and jointly created viable, adaptable systems and legal frameworks on a 🌍 🌍 🌍 basis, giving decentralized, local structures the space to maintain and create highly diverse models of co-existing.

Technology and big data helped us to turn new and old ideas into reality. And often architects were part of the denouements because they had answers instead of coming up with more questions. Drama is now history. We live in a radical democracy, in a radical bureaucracy. On a planet that doesn't know or need heroes or villains.

German Pavilion at the
17th International Architecture Exhibition
— La Biennale di Venezia

we started mimicking the algorithms and the technologies that the big players were using

2038, *A Crisis in Architecture?*

Diana Alvarez-Marin, *coding, changing, learning*

Sorry, 2038!

Sorry, that's the best we can do at the moment. Not everything is perfect. There are still some idiots running around doing bad things. But only a few. And anyway, we can afford them! Yes, we are far from paradise, but we live in a much better world than 15 or 20 years ago.

How? With new and old ideas. With a certain systemic robustness that we have built up over the last 15 years. We designed ourselves out of disaster. Because we started to think it all together.

When, in 2020, the pandemic broke out, we could feel the crisis simultaneously everywhere. Yes, feel. Unlike the climate catastrophe, inequality, or migration, which only some people have faced, the pandemic was felt by everyone. Grief, fear, pity, pain, loneliness. Suddenly emotions were shared. Drama was universal.

Before that, we'd lost touch with the world. We'd lost the feeling for the whole. That changed suddenly. Kim Stanley Robinson wrote back then: "September 11th was a single day, and everyone felt the shock of it, but our daily habits didn't shift, except at airports; the President even urged us to keep shopping. This crisis is different. It's a biological threat, and it's global. Everyone has to change together to deal with it. That's really history."

That was in the beginning. When everyone thought there might be a way back. As if everything was better before. Then came the big economic crisis. Whole states imploded. That had many reasons, too.

In 2023, a short moment of calm followed. Like after an attack. As if mankind had come to its senses. There was a collective insight that we need contracts and systems that keep adapting to an infinitely surprising, fluctuating and ever-changing environment. That there are no technological solutions, but that technology can help us to revive old ideas. Like Stafford Beer's Viable System Model. And the fears, cell phones, mites, clouds, dreams, viruses, utopias, AIs and fairy tales did the rest.

And now slowly, very slowly, we are starting to get a feeling for the world again. Because we learned from Buckminster Fuller see also page 110 that we should work less on a singular future and more on an endless scenario universe of connections, joints, interstices, and storylines. Like Sultana Scheherazade in *One Thousand and One Nights* kept designing worlds of coexistence to escape death.

We managed to deal with complexity. Because we stopped changing people and instead built adaptable, viable systems. Locally and globally. Decentralised and centralised. We have built functioning bureaucracies in most parts of the world, which are constantly changing. And which, in conjunction with humans and non-humans and their personal AIs, give new opportunities not only for participation but also for protection. They really help. Every child nowadays dreams of becoming a bureaucrat. Nobody wants a tattoo or a t-shirt of Che Guevara anymore — everybody wants a portrait of Max Weber.

system, roundabout, *complexity*

Mara Balestrini, *orchestrated (eco)systems*

Looking Backward: 2038–2021

Jacob Eli Goldman

"Ideas improve. The meaning of words participates."
Comte de Lautréamont, *Poésies*

It's 2038, but I'm writing in the period language of 2021, so far as I remember it. By language, I don't mean any one in particular, but the medium in which meaning is made and remade; and by this odd conceit, I don't mean to over-complicate anything, but to clarify an already complicated subject, which is this: the role played by language in the making of the present, ours in particular — 2038.[1]

Before proceeding, let me justify my method. To do so, I must first state the obvious: the world has changed considerably in the past two decades. But it hasn't changed all of a sudden. Nor has it changed so dramatically as to make the past unrecognizable in the eyes of the present, evidenced by the fact that these words, the ones I'm writing, are familiar and not altogether meaningless. Indeed, these words suggest an unmistakable continuity between past and present. Not that anyone claims otherwise. But this continuity is deceiving — a point to which I'll later return.[2] For now, suffice it to repeat: the world has changed, and yet much has stayed the same.

My method — I admit it's indirect. Why not address the role of language in the present using, well, language of the present? This could certainly be done, and done straight-forwardly. But here ease would come at the cost of effect. For if I am to substantiate what I believe — that the changes which together amount to the present cannot be explained, nor even really be understood, without confronting cor-responding shifts in language — then I'm buoyed by the following protection: where my method fails, where the language of 2021 can't account for the conditions of 2038, is precisely where the method is most instructive. That is, if the present is unmistakably distinct from the past, then dressing the former in the clothes of its adolescence will reveal the contours of this distinction. And where the seams begin to break is where this conceit of mine is working.

A quick look at the fundamental mutability of language might serve to avoid abstraction. In 1962, George Kluber wrote in *The Shape of Time* of what was then a recent finding: taking into account vocabularies and official definitions therein, cognate languages drift at a fixed rate from their common root. This trajectory assures us that, if language is persistent, it is not unchanging. But what makes language flexible is also what makes it possible to commandeer, and in ways whose effects are less subject to the accounting of statistical analysis. Far more slippery than dictionary definitions are the connotations and metaphors which together compose what might be called the affective dimension of language. While this is of course the realm of aesthetics, it is also that of politics. Examples of the latter include the many instances of totalitarian takeovers of language, epitomized by Newspeak in Orwell's *1984*, when unsuspecting words and phrases begin to act as coded veils for violent ideologies, until the two become indistinguishable (e.g. 'reeducate' → 'put to death'). From the perspective of political opposition, consider how in 1970's Britain and South Africa, anti-racist and anti-apartheid activists used 'Black' to designate a range of minority ethnicities in an effort to expand solidary against white domination. On the one hand, language is used to normalize violence; on the other, to manifest broad coalitions of resistance or to establish codes of subversion under the guise of compliance.

16

In both cases, words are made to mean more than they say, and to do so within particular combinations of social, political, cultural, and historical contexts. This—the fact that meaning is both variable and highly conditional—is the essential point, for it reveals that, not only is language as a whole unfixed, but each language, each tongue, contains within it countless others which are on the surface one, but in terms of the meaning they produce, many. That this diversity of meaning is so often inseparable from conflict is what brings us to the significance of the particular conditions of 2038, where such antagonisms are conspicuously absent—not, it must be said, on account of having shed language and the multiplicity of meaning therein, but of having, as it were, made good on it. And this is remarkable.

Now, what are these conditions? By the skin of our teeth we have overcome crisis after crisis to achieve a radically democratic, radically bureaucratic, international, decentralized, redistributive order, in which animals see also page 231 and ecosystems alike are enfranchised, which is to say, united with us as equal entities, equal constituents in this great balancing act that has, for now, all the makings of being (with no small degree of consensus) a new serenity. This is how 2038 looks in the language of a time when some of these changes were taking root, others were well under way, and still others were all but inconceivable. The question, again, is what part language played, and continues to play, in all of this.

My answer, which finds echoes throughout history, from the Kabbalists to the great cultural materialists of the last century, is this: the institutions that make 2038 what it is—*this* direct democracy, *this* automated bureaucracy, *this* international politics, *this* empathic individualism (if the two words are irreconcilable, it is individualism, not empathy, that's now absent)—these institutions are, essentially, linguistic constructions. Far from claiming that their being so makes them somehow unreal, it is rather that their reality becomes meaningful according to how they're articulated, and that the possibilities of any articulation, any utterance, are limited by *what* is meaningful *when* (and *where*).[3] In other words, if these institutions are, not necessarily entirely new, but at least different from their precedents, it can only be on account of their being constructed within a new, or different, constellation of meaning, which for its part comprises the possibilities for how these institutions can operate. Of course, this doesn't mean that our institutions are themselves passive, but that they're subject to what meaning makes of them, just as meaning clings to whatever comes its way. Which is to say that meaning is shaped by particular conditions, conditions which become discernable only through the meaning they produce.

The implications of this dynamic relation between meaning and the conditions of its making are, for our purposes, thus: in 2038, to have reconceived of what constitutes that which, in 2021, was called an individual or a nation (to take but two examples from above), is to have overcome whatever conditions accounted for either's former meaning, which has since changed. see also page 237 That is, 2038 is possible thanks to a new set of meanings that, like all others, reveal the conditions from which they were forged. Put another way, for a term like 'nation' to signify something other than what it did in 2021, when rampant nationalisms persisted, suggests that the meaning such conditions produced has since been liquidated, made over, or extended, now that the conditions have changed. (And the ways in which 'nation' has come to be understood are, I want to propose, part of what makes the particular international formation of the new serenity possible.)

I said these changes didn't happen overnight. But eighteen years is not so long either. Indeed, what's transpired over the course of them would make a period twice as long seem tumultuous. For this *vivace*, we have crisis to thank, since it is in times of crisis when meaning is most subject to change, and subject to change most rapidly. The Black Death turned the deadly sins into virtues overnight; it also compelled the resurgence of classical values that would result in the Renaissance. Further examples abound. In any case, that so much has changed so quickly is all the more reason to suspect that some of the seeds of meaning that constitute 2038 are embedded within these very words.[4] Though the words themselves haven't much changed. Yes, perhaps we now have newer ones which I'm loath to use here, this being the language of 2021, but it can hardly be expected that one vocabulary would supplant another. Instead, what happened, what always happens, is that under the cover of nominal continuity, words acquired new meanings without losing their old ones. Just as Freud described the mind as capable of containing in the present the ruins of its past, so it is with language. Meaning proliferates, but does so discreetly, while the word looks on blankly, giving no indication of the activity it contains. To listen closely, however, is to remember that the word is not a neutral, ahistorical sign, but an unsuspecting agent of change. Like a crab that grows without shedding its shell, meaning shifts while the word for it remains.

'Nation', 'individual' — we still say both. And to make matters more confusing, their definitions haven't much changed. But their relevance, their use, has been altered: no longer does either concept exist as an end in itself, as it once did; neither national interests nor individual ones are any longer primary, now that both nations and individuals exist for other nations, other individuals. Lest we relapse into the sort of crises we were only so lucky to overcome, we speak now of individuals and nations with a memory and understanding of the roles they may have played in our descent. So, if their meanings have changed — and they can't but change — it is first of all because both words are used in a time that no longer suits them, now as artifacts, timestamped, as it were, by history. In the end, we can still speak (indeed, are speaking) of the present in language that precedes it, but not without what Borges calls "a certain affectation," a certain affectation which indicates a historical displacement, a historical displacement which is always meaningful.

To accept the role of language in the making of the present is to admit that the present will soon be past. This is so for precisely the same reason that it sometimes seems otherwise: language changes under cover, so to speak, and so evades suspicion even as its effects become apparent. Indeed, this durability — the persistence of words and the rules by which they're combined — is what makes the tongues of 2021 legible in 2038. But it is also what allows the conditionality of meaning to be forgotten, and with it, the fact that it is through us, mere speakers of language, that meaning takes hold. Thus, we can thank ourselves for 2038, but we might be wary of the words we use to do so, and the effects, intended or not, they might have.

A final note: At the end of Calvino's *Invisible Cities,* Marco Polo comes to the unjust city of Berenice. Within it, he finds a hidden city, that of the just, and deeper still, a seed of injustice bred from the resentment of those who consider themselves to be most just of all. "From my words," says the explorer, "you will have reached the conclusion that the real Berenice is a temporal succession of different cities, alternately just and unjust. But what I wanted to warn you about is something else: all the future Berenices are already present in this instant, wrapped one within the other, confined, crammed, inextricable." This cautionary tale might also be applied to language, within which the future—both its and ours—is latent.

1 English—and my particular use of it—being but one manifestation of this medium of meaning, I use it neither arrogantly nor suggestively, but simply as a matter of necessity: then (2021), as now (2038), it is the only language I really know; and certainly the only one I know well enough to carry out this conceit of anachronism. Not only could this all be done just as well in another language, but a variety of linguistic perspectives is necessary for the subject to be addressed comprehensively.

2 An example of the deceit of this continuity at work: Julian West, the protagonist of Edward Bellamy's Looking Backward 2000-1887, falls into a deep sleep and awakes more than a century later. When he does, he slips right into conversation with those who find him. He's dazed, but through words alone is given no sense of the dramatic material changes he'll soon behold.

3 Susanne Langer: "... language grows in meaning by a process of articulation ..."

4 Merleau-Ponty: "A language sometimes remains a long time pregnant with transformations which are to come."

2023

Today, 1350 employees of BlackRock's risk management subsidiary called BR-Solutions were fired after having been found guilty by the New York Supreme Court. They were charged with being responsible for the manipulation of data which was fed into the data analysis system named Aladdin.

I Love my Time 💕 2038 💕

Christopher Roth

(astro)logical advisor: Olaf Grawert

Omoju Miller & Audrey Tang, *Surfin'2*

Het is zondag
In spring 2035, you see shopping bags everywhere that return themselves to the store after being used, origami-ing themselves into butterflies. Invented more than 25 years ago by William Gibson.

In 2026, Uber and Lyft were taken over by their employees and became worker coops. A cooperatively owned network of drivers now set pay rates and work rules democratically.

Montag
It's summer. The negotiations start on June 8, 2027, and most of the world is connected: Geneva, Montreal, Maputo, Taipei, Brasilia, Rome, Tel-Aviv, Baghdad. Proposals for new modes of organizing, fundamental geo- and cosmo-political rights, and legal frameworks are on the table now. Ready to be discussed and streamlined. The idea is to collectively establish viable, adaptable systems on a planetary basis, giving decentralised, local structures the space to maintain and create highly diverse models of co-existing. That work for human and non-human subjects at the same time. That are about observation, measurement and experience. That look at the real world where the action is, where real people live under real constraints. Systems that repair themselves. Models that last. For a hundred years? Or more?

On the 8th of June 2027, Uranus was in Gemini — an auspicious time for new ideas. When the two encounter, innovation and revolution meet information and transmission. Of new creations and unknown technology. But Gemini has two faces and their Mercury casts a shadow on

Uranus! Intellect vs. feeling. This we learned. No success without emotions. How do we build a world that works but does not exclude affects and emotions? We had to take the chance. Erik Bordeleau, one of the architects of the contracts, remembers: "We experimented with Moten's and Harney's Fugitive Planning. Precarious, transductive, ecstatic planning. The type deployed by a self-effacing radical bureaucracy. This was about transforming fundamentally what it means—for anyone, really—to be 'part of the system' and changing the structure of feeling usually associated with it."

Emotions mean uncertainty, but based on necessary decisions made by the mind. And by autonomous systems. We are in a constant process of snatching emergent order out of affect. What does it mean at a collective, psycho-political level? How do you feedback contingency into open-ended systems? How do you feedback feelings into ecologically-infused planning? Seek advice! Spirited, assertive and energetic women will help. They may tell you that uncertainty (and the backfiring that results) sometimes 'make sense'.

The negotiations lasted four years and 18 days. They were tough but fruitful. The spirited and energetic women helped. The complexity of the system (many still refuse to use the word 'system') and its subsystems is enormous. But nobody has to know or understand all of it. It is decentralised within the planetary framework and the subsystems are more or less autonomous. Only when the confused signals of subsystemic problems reach a higher level in the overall system do centralised councils (of humans and nonhumans) intervene. Joanna Pope, another important architect of the frameworks: "The challenge has been to figure out what technologies we want to keep and which ones are just too socially and ecologically detrimental in everyday arrangements and everyday life to keep maintaining. Now both, bottom-up and top-down processes have to work together to end the artificial scarcity that capitalism created."

Information about environmental, social, and economic conditions are collected and monitored by the public and by governments on all levels as continuously and promptly as possible. Fast-responding, self-regulating, self-organizing. E. Glen Weyl, responsible for social tech in the negotiations: "There has been a major change in attitude from the local scale to the global scale. The whole point of these social technologies is that they allow us to reproduce more of the features of life in small communities in the broad world."

We included environmental and social costs in prices and indicators, so that there is no confusion about the consequences. see also page 83 This makes the entire system and all of its layers adaptable, robust and viable.

And here we are. Everything is ready to be signed, on the 26th of June, 2031. Jupiter stands for abundance and generosity. This giant planet fuels all kinds of positive optimism in our lives and is considered to be the planet of miracles, of hope and opportunity. In cancer, Jupiter is exalted, which means that all its good qualities are maximized. Loyalty, justice, fairness, balance, judgment, incorruptibility. Very rarely is there a day under such a clear vision: of equity, fairness and objectivity. And on this very day the contracts and legal agreements that are mutually beneficial to all parties are signed. Erik Bordeleau in 2031: "For we are always already at stake with each other, partnered all the way down. Inhabitants of the world, earthlings and earthbounds, creatures of all kinds, human and non-human, we are entangled in a series of interlaced trails and creative feedback loops, holding open life for one another. In the world to come, everyone holds pieces of each other's life, socially and financially. We are entre-preneurs and entre-donneurs, inter-holders and inter-givers, networked together to collectively distribute the risks and opportunities of living." see also page 101

Es martes

July 14, 2037. A man and a woman in bed surrounded by trees, which serve as both facade and roof. The woman's name is Toni. Toni wears glasses. She gently ruffles the man's fake grey hair. (You can spray your hair daily these days.) The man is called Radek and has his head on her fake breasts. (You can put on different fake breasts, penises and bottoms weekly at most. More frequent changes would be bad for the metabolism.) Radek looks at the ceiling. The sun shines through the large trees and you hear some goats from the other side. Toni speaks with a German accent. Radek's speech is unaccented, though he uses Eastern slang.

Toni: We care.
Radek: Sure we do.
Toni: For the first time in history we live in a system that cares.
Radek: I know.
Toni: It wasn't easy after all.
Radek: No, it wasn't.
He looks at her, smiles.
Radek: Are you preparing your speech?
Toni *(smiles back)*: The crises taught as a lesson.

28

Radek: Is that the title?

Toni: No it isn't. We can't just talk about the crisis. It's over.

Radek: But you do.

Toni: Well, only as a ramp. A story ramp.

Radek: Okay. Where does it ramp to?

Toni: It's about the economy, about redistribution of wealth and resources.

She looks at the alarm clock.

Toni: Shit, do I really have to meet the French President today?

Radek: No, she can wait. That's fine, she was anyway going to Hannover to see some old comrades.

Toni: By herself?

Radek: Think so.

Toni: Shouldn't we go with her?

Radek: Didn't you just say, you don't want to see her?

Toni: Yeah. I'm undecided.

Radek: We have time. Just slack. Tell me where the crisis ramps us up to.

Toni: Okay I'll cut the crisis.

Radek: No, you need a ramp. True. An intro, an exposition.

Toni: But people know anyway. People know of the crisis and of the good things which came out of it. So why giving a speech in the first place?

Radek: Well, people doubt. It hasn't been very long that things go well. They need to trust.

Toni: True.

Radek: What speeches do you like in general?

Toni: I like Bria talking.

Radek: Yes. Pragmatic. Transatlantic. Very cool.

Toni: Morozov is more enthusiastic.

Radek: The one he gave at the Beer thing?

Toni: That was epic.

Radek: How long was it?

Toni: Like ten hours?

Radek: Only Fidel Castro and Buckminster Fuller could do more.

Toni: According to Wigley, Fuller was wearing special NASA diapers because he didn't want to make breaks.

Radek: That's hilarious. So what is your speech about?

Toni: Common, let's go to Hannover and have cake with Marie-Claire.

Radek: No! Speech first.

Toni: Okay, it is about solidarity and empathy. Because in the crisis, when asked whom to leave behind to maintain the status quo, we..., we all kind of went: 'no one at all!'

Radek: Did we? Nice.

Toni: But this had to be encrypted into our model or into our system. We needed this to be systemic. Not to appeal to the good in each individual.

Radek: No, that didn't work.

Toni: No holding hands and preaching and morals and that kind of shit...

Radek: You sound like Schumacher.

Toni: Even the broken clock is right twice a day...

Radek: Common, he is better than that.

Toni: I know, joking. So solidarity had to be inscribed into the meta-system. I mean it goes kind of back to Beer.

Radek: It goes back to Fuller.

Toni: And to Ostrom...

Radek: What's your speech for again?
Toni: teen-vogue.tv
Radek: Cool.
Toni: They are the best!
Radek: Let's go to Hannover then, I'm hungry too.

Nous sommes mercredi

For four years now, Oana takes four selfies per day. Ongoing. Today, on the 2nd of February 2028, she will take number 4508, number 9,10 and 11. Mostly close-ups. Sometimes she takes medium-shots from her left side in a mirror. Oana prefers her left side. Like Audrey Hepburn did. She puts on a skirt over her fake bottom. The skirt is Italian, the bottom Irish. Looks slinky. 4508. Her body didn't really change much in the last 10 years. These photographs all come with a political message: "The economy cannot be separated from ecology!" or "We are in this together!" 4509. 4510 is a detail of her left toe: "The global challenges cannot be solved nationally." One more to go. The selfies are trojan horses. Oana doesn't trust the silence. The negotiations have been dragging on for half a year now. She is involved. But not really. Not enough. Sometimes she calls the ceasefire 'boredom.' No drama. No heroes. No villains. How can we trust this? She was in too many fights. Romania was a mess. Like a stranded whale at the shores of the 2020s. Oana was paralysed. The super star from the Carpathian Mountains of Transylvania. She founded a party. She was sitting on the fence. Between the old left autocracy and a centre technocrat decentralised movement. She kept explaining, talking, discussing. Soon her allies were drunk from power and easy to buy over. At the same time Oana Bogdan was a very successful architect in Brussels. With a golden business card. On the fence. Oana

green feminist digital cities

2037

The global challenges cannot be solved nationally

2028

The economy cannot be separated from ecology!

2028

33

doesn't age, like none of Bela Lugosi's daughters do. It's a Wednesday. 4511. And it is Groundhog Day. Tomorrow will be 4512–4515.

In 2028, George Clooney, Tulsi Gabbard, Serena Williams, Roger Federer, Miley Cyrus, and Jay-Z, among many others, renounced much of their property. Even the Catholic Church made its land available. But charity was not the solution. We installed a permanent redistribution of wealth into the system. Taxes for instance are an unbeatable equalizing mechanism to break the loop of the rich getting richer and the poor getting poorer.

今天是星期四

Remember the 2nd of March 2023? The ego-driven Sun aligned with retrograde Neptune. Neptune was there to help us detach from our ego and consciousness and exist in the in-between. The fall from arrogance to humility. The collapse of the ego came with a radical change in our world-view and values. Often this collapse is triggered by a sudden event.

There are a few theories how this happened. From what we know, the 'Jackpot' see also page 83 and 91, an expression coined by William Gibson as the "long-duration apocalypse," started in the early 1980s and accelerated during the pandemic. After that, we were used to horror news. We stopped counting the swans. Black, green, pink, whatever colour was appointed to them. Our socio-economic system became unmanageable. We had overshot our limits.

It's the 2nd of March 2023. What a date: 2323 or 3223. It's a cold Thursday in Tokyo and in Frankfurt, rain in

Singapore, Dakar and New York. At 11am Eastern Tir ,
Aladdin, BlackRock's risk management platform and the
world's largest realtime-money-managing-operating system classifies China as 'ultra high risk.' What had happened? After the pandemic, China, with all its big-shot
projects, maintained the illusion of economic success. But
by 2021, the Communist party celebrated its centenary
with parades and celebrations while most of their debtors
around the world were insolvent. And by 2022, China's
money engine began to stutter a little too loud. BlackRock
fed Aladdin with contradicting data to prevent the self-fulfilling prophecies. But Aladdin has a 360-degree perspective with its robot-advisers and immense data processing.
It withdrew its trust. China's crisis reinforced. Things
collapsed into a vicious circle. Exactly like in Aladdin's
scenario. This was the beginning of act 3 of the Jackpot and
its climax. The following weeks were hit by major world-
wide financial losses, by collapsing markets and regions.
And at the same time anything was possible now. We had
won a chance to re-organise on a bigger scale. Within the
meltdown we discovered the ideal conditions for changing
the feedback structure and the information links. The old
chain of command, the authoritarian hierarchies, and the
corrupt elites became useless and had to go. For good.

15 years later we choose our representatives mostly by
sortition (by lot) and gaming. Along with quadratic voting,
that is, measuring the degree of preferences, rather than just
the direction, gaming proved to be a serious alternative to
the one-person-one-vote (1p1v) principle. We use sortition
to minimise factionalism and to represent a spectrum. We
use QV to mirror efficiently the preferences of a larger
population because QV is simple and robust. 1p1v is mostly

Spaceship Earth

used on a communal level, for smaller policies and less popular topics. With gaming and Massively Multiplayer Online Games (MMOs) we run crowdsourced simulations. Data is not used for control but for participation. And gaming has a lot to do with emotions. Good games are good stories. Today MMOs play a key role in governance. Competing policy proposals are gamed in parallel. This made us more flexible and faster in redesigning physical and social systems. Sometimes games collapse and gamers join more viable games until the best proposal is played through by all. The game is a surrogate ballot, the majority position serving as a binding decision. Through gaming and Viable System Models we successfully accelerated our response times when the environment or the society is stressed (affect & emotions!). Most problems today are forecast before they appear. Many architects became gamers since gaming is part of their education now. It extends the planning horizon. Options are based on long-term costs and benefits, not just on market or election results. *How Do We Want to Live Together?* is a bestseller-game that got many more people interested in the wellbeing of the population and the impact of human activity on the world ecosystem.

QV, sortition and especially gaming broke some gridlocks undermining our democracies. Richard Buckminster Fuller experimented with game mechanics and envisioned a so-called World Game. see also page 110 The game's objective was "to make the world work for 100% of humanity in the shortest possible time through spontaneous cooperation without ecological offence or the disadvantage of anyone." The ultimate goal of the system was to make everyone a winner.

It's Friday
Oil is dead!

É sábado
"… the past is still very much in the present: the present is merely the past which has survived the algorithm's natural selection. Whilst the tree-story ascends in complexity, the ancient horizontal base is here and now. The hyperstitional 'call to the old ones' is surely an attempt to establish a communicative link with this base, or to re-hijack the immense cunning and plasticity of the base … As far as I see it, hyperstition is obsessed with the impact of virtual futures on the psychotechno-capitalist infrastructure of the present, whether those futures take the shape of utopian goals or nightmarish catastrophes … History is crucial because it is littered with the wreckage of failed hyperstitional projects …" Nick Land, *Hyperstition Laboratory*.

"Planning rests on the idea that time is not instantaneous but continuous. A wellplotted plan has more to do with binge watching a TV show than a distracted online presence. The recent rise of TV culture proves that a planned and cultivated stretch of time can be adequately thrilling to stimulate an utopian impulse. A compelling economic SciFi is mathematics disguised in a well-crafted storyline." Bahar Noorizadeh, *After Scarcity*.

Сегодня воскресенье
Last Sunday, Patrik sat, feeling quite relaxed, in a cafe in Covent Garden and talked to a former student from Austria. She is Minister of Agriculture now, one of the many architects who went into politics and bureaucracy, a trajectory that Patrik was responsible for in part. When asked about

his rowdy past, he tells us that many of his demands were impulses that put us on the path where we stand. Liberland? Has provoked very important discussions. "If enough people buy into it, it starts to matter. But it wasn't all that serious." He was trying to get the left out of their trivial factional infighting, he says. The eternal battle of identities. Always criticism, never progress. In the end, even Michael Moore was their enemy. Schumacher was the founder of the Stop-Holding Hands movement in the late 2020s. He always believed in systems. Niklas Luhmann is his reference. He always thought big. But when it came to urban development, he only ever looked to the economic side of it and to growth. The question was: How much planning, solidarity and non-human feedback would the libertarian ideology allow? Schumacher was part of the negotiations in the late 2020s. He came with optimal demands. In the end, however, there was more Murray Bookchin in the results than he had thought. Now Schumacher is Mayor of London and the city is doing well. Even the mayor of a metropolis has not so much influence anymore. Because there are planetary frameworks, but more important, a lot of power comes — bottom-up — from the districts. The districts also own the land. And Ealing is organized in a completely different way to Hackney. They even have different currencies. And it works! Covent Garden with its piazzas is the closest to Liberland. Who would have thought that London would become a green-digital-feminist city? And that Patrik would be so relaxed about it.

E' lunedì
… I learn do it yourself cybernetics
while I'm jogging on a rolling tray
I love my weekends in the pure air

on the heights of the Eiffel tower
My time my time I love my time
My time has something more
My time's the best there's ever been
My time I love my time
Thank you my time…

From *My Time* by Ann Steel & Roberto Cacciapaglia. Covered by Telex one year later.

Monday, May 24, 2038. In Venice. At the Giardini. Three Nazis full of cheap Schnapps and dressed in mini-skirts dance around the German Pavilion. They celebrate the centenary of Hitler coming to Venice for the reopening of the pavilion in 1938. Yes, we still have a few nazis. There are still bad people around.

It's like E. Glen Weyl said recently: "It's like in Star Trek. People are still messed up and imperfect and all sorts of bad things happen. But it's also clearly a much better world. In some pretty profound and radical ways. But there's no sense in which we've reached anything like Nirvana."

And here, thinking of Venice, from *The German Ideology*: "The 'essence' of the fish is its 'being', water… The 'essence' of the freshwater fish is the water of a river. But the latter ceases to be the 'essence' of the fish and is no longer a suitable medium of existence as soon as the river is made to serve industry, as soon as it is polluted by dyes and other waste products and navigated by steamboats, or as soon as its water is diverted into canals where simple drainage can deprive the fish of its medium of existence." see also page 231 Here Marx and Engels argue that "the uneasiness of a single creature in the world is not a problem only for this particular creature but for the world itself," as Oxana Timofeeva reminds us.

今日は火曜日だ．

Pluto and Uranus are having a power struggle. Luckily this is rare. Pluto is the planet of death, sex, and transformation. Beneath the surface. While the energetic Uranus is determined to overcome any obstacle. Ever heard of the Age of Aquarius? 1960s' peaceful protesters? They all had Uranus in Aquarius. Questioning authority and championing individuality. Characteristics of Uranus. 02.11.2032. The stars say this Tuesday in November is decision day. Tulsi Gabbard vs. Keller Easterling. Who is Pluto and who is Uranus? Gabbard would be the first female combat veteran as president. Pluto! But she is a Hindu, a surfer and an early supporter of Medicare for All, always endorsed Universal Basic Income and opposed military interventionism. Uranus! On the other side Keller Easterling, who, some years ago said she would be ready for the job but doesn't know if she has the charisma. Who needs charisma nowadays to be president? There is much less light on POTUS than 15 years ago. Tulsi vs. Keller is really about expertise and knowledge. V. Mitch McEwen: "I guess it was when Keller Easterling was first in the primaries that we started to see briefs about Housing and Urban Development." And this was key! Mark Wigley: "You have to remember, she was never quite an architect. Her training was in theater. Keller comes from theater. I think she had the advantage of not being an architect. So for her, the post architectural world was sort of obvious and natural. Those lessons, the Easterling lessons for infrastructure, were like rethinking infrastructure." Tulsi became the Vice-president. In a way, there are no antago-nists anymore. Pluto is in a relationship. Death, sex, and transformation are all fine.

Het is weer woensdag.
In 1971, Heinz von Foerster prefaced his article *Perception of the Future and the Future of Perception* with the prophetic quote from composer Herbert Brün: "The definition of a problem and the action taken to solve it largely depend on the view which the individuals or groups that discov-ered the problem have of the system to which it refers. A problem may thus find itself defined as a badly interpreted output, or as a faulty output of a faulty output device, or as a faulty output due to a malfunction in an otherwise faultless system, or as a correct but undesired output from a faultless and thus undesirable system. All definitions but the last suggest corrective action; only the last definition suggests change, and so presents an unsolvable problem to anyone opposed to change"

È di nuovo giovedì
After four successful years, President Easterling had handed over to her successor V. Mitch McEwen. Another architect! Although presidents are becoming less impor-tant, both are among the most popular incumbents of all time. McEwen still has half of her first term to go. She can take it pretty easy; most things seem to be working themselves out by now. In her speech last Saturday, Jan. 1, 2039, she spoke of "systemic robustness" that we've been building for the past 15 years.

Keller Easterling, *History Channel*

V. Mitch McEwen, *the reparations*

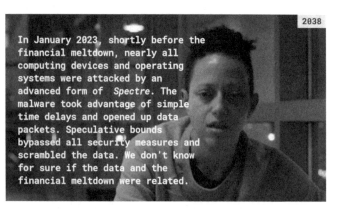

In January 2023, shortly before the
financial meltdown, nearly all
computing devices and operating
systems were attacked by an
advanced form of *Spectre*. The
malware took advantage of simple
time delays and opened up data
packets. Speculative bounds
bypassed all security measures and
scrambled the data. We don't know
for sure if the data and the
financial meltdown were related.

2038

2038

the meltdown
in 2023

V. Mitch McEwen, *the reparations*

V. Mitch McEwen, *the reparations*

V. Mitch McEwen, 2028, *coding, changing, learning*

2023

Today, the stock price of the Export-Import Bank of the Republic of China dropped by 268%. The Bank had been offering credit insurance to various big-shot real estate projects in foreign countries, which were cancelled after the Aladdin affair.

Sketches from a Secession

Erica Love and João Enxutu

America was bitterly divided by the time Covid-19 struck in early 2020. The rupture had been triggered by political indifference, the wealth gap, crackpot conspiracies, the 9/11 attacks, Bush v. Gore, the Civil War, chattle slavery, and so on ... Over the first two decades of the 21st century the breaches to civil society had become particularly acute and persistent. Volatility, which fueled the finance and media industries, simply became too intense and debilitating. The endless churn of viral proxy wars battered whatever was left to prop up the Union. Once the pandemic blew through, the house of cards collapsed decisively.

At this point you have been staying in place for over a month, in some cases longer. If you are among those fortunate enough to be at home with a reliable internet connection the view of the United States through your computer terminal has, at times, been terrifying. We can assure you, however, that the quarantines will end and that something good and meaningful is waiting on the other side.

The "Liberate" media events that you recently witnessed launched open conflicts between the states and federal government which became irreconcilable. Demonstrators delivered demands for the right to work at the door of state houses occupied by Democratic governors. These events, to a large degree, were cases of astroturfing boosted by the President on Twitter. "Operation Gridlock" was designed for maximum exposure. Handmade signs read: "Trust in Jesus not the New World Order," "Don't Tread on Me," and "I need a haircut." Photographs of brave hospital workers blocking the paths of menacing

Dodge and Ford trucks have become iconic: an American knock-off of the Tiananmen Square standoff.

With distance, reckless demands and deplorable tactics by protestors could be boiled down to a struggle for human rights. In America basic provisions were tied to a job. A business lockdown, in effect, cut access to social safety. Work continued nonetheless. As high-earning cognitive labor struggled with screen fatigue, essential workers (who were disproportionately people of color) continued to risk their lives on the front-lines. As Jordan Flowers, an Amazon warehouse worker put it, "How can we be 'essential' and 'disposable' at the same time?"[1] On March 30 of 2020 Flowers, with 50 of his co-workers, staged a walkout at their Staten Island facility. America had promised jobs as a cure; they became the disease instead.

Record unemployment led millions to lose their health-care in the middle of the pandemic. Strikes, walkouts, and sickouts intensified as the summer wore on. Covid-19 cases surged and remained persistently high as gridlock in the federal government prevented a financial stimulus from reaching businesses and individuals. Outrage, dulled by prolonged isolation, turned into existential rage once it was given space in the streets. Social justice struggles took center stage and "Black Lives Matter" became the largest movement in the nation's history.

As public health and other essential professionals worked tirelessly to limit the scope of the disaster, others tempered anxieties by mapping possibilities beyond what was imminently knowable. This tendency was certainly evident in the art field, where cooped up imaginations fluctuated wildly from the most dire endgame scenarios to vital expressions of solidarity that extended well beyond the arts.

In the early weeks, speculation about the future of Contemporary Art in the U.S. was generally grim. Countless, deeply-felt reflections circulated across publishing platforms. There was time to read. The takes were wide-raging but even among those who shared cultural affinities differences could be plotted mostly along generational lines. Some of the older commentariat who came of age in the 1970's, during New York City's bad old days, imagined that by having borne witness to one period of bust and boom, prosperity would gradually return to those who could wait it out with "Passion. Obsession. Desire."[2] A devotion to cyclical history helped in no small way to confirm fools in their faith. The economic unraveling of the 1970s was not a reboot event but the conjuncture of a new regime known as neoliberalism.

Difference and density were impediments to the recasting of New York City in the aseptic modernist mold that was favored after the World Wars. The city proved not to be a pliable enough medium for the "master builders" and after decades of neglect by white elites the city was left for dead. And, so, it was with passion, obsession, and desire that a small community of artists in the 1970s resettled the wasted metropolis and delivered great American art from out of the deprivation. The scrappy bunch which occupied abandoned lofts in

Lower Manhattan were the germ for an expansion that by 2020 had mushroomed into a multi-billion dollar global industry. In its final years the old art market became so bloated with ancillary prestige events (galas, fairs, etc...) staged in fealty to oligarch patrons that these satellite affairs ended up swallowing the planet which they orbited. In those days much vibrancy, critical energy, and transformative potential was squandered in beating back influencers, sorting through outrage, and paying the rent. Even now, 18 years on, we can't help but indulge in a bump of recollections drawn from your lurid milieu.

Let's continue with the fallout: Museums, theaters, and galleries that closed in mid-March remained shut for months. In all, the infrastructure that furnished live public spectatorship went dark for longer than most could have anticipated. Contemporary art galleries attenuated by market strain for too long, staged mergers or simply folded. Hopes for a sustainable market rebound sparked by an ascendant patron class of conscious-capitalists that would source locally-grown artists from emerging galleries never materialized. [3] The human compulsion to possess singular commodities is a difficult force to regulate.

The dominos continued to fall when it became clear that there would not be a federal bailout of the nonprofit arts sector. In the years leading up to Covid-19 there was very little public provision to shore things up to begin with; the National Endowment of the Arts had been threatened with elimination four years running. What had been starved for decades would be the first to perish. For their part, arts foundations joined together to provide relief, but the economic impact of the virus was too widespread and too sustained. Payments were furnished for immediate support — a bridge, it was hoped, to somewhere.

Young Americans subsisting on a precarious creative economy before the pandemic were quickly forced to redirect their energies to the fundamentals of survival. These abrupt introductions to urban immiseration prompted a hunt for alternatives. The Great Depression was the obvious historical precedent and texts covering the New Deal's Federal Arts Project (FAP) began appearing on Zoom reading group lists. In sustained examinations of bygone post office mural paintings advocated by federal administrators named Holger Cahill and Rexford Tugwell, the fog of 85 years became all the more dense. Artists of the Great Depression had made concessions to decorate and propagandize for a wage — to bear the yoke of social realism and the remit of FAP administrators to update the conventions of Americana. In those years — for the sake of self-preservation — American artists were forced to redefine their output as craft. As your contemporary Dave Beech notes, the Euro-American artist since the Renaissance had couched their exceptionalism within the "aristocratic project of the eradication of labour within labour itself." He explains further, "This is how it was possible for art to pass itself off from the outset as unteachable, immeasurable, spontaneous, and free from rules." [4] It would follow that a demand for a subsidy in times of economic crisis would require that the artist again shed their claim to exceptionalism. see also page 189

With a measure of historical perspective some in the art field recalibrated their approach to movement politics. Allegiances between art workers and broader labor movements were cultivated like never before, but the internet had forever muddied the waters of what constituted creative labor. To this day unruly armies of humans and bots push out countless disintermediation schemes, deep fakes, and shit posts: All of which became tactically valuable when the time came for the secession. However, Franklin Delano Roosevelt's messianic return never came.

What we now call the Soft Secession was not a single revolutionary event but rather an escalation brought on by the collapse of the U.S. and global economies after Covid-19 and the 2020 election which was plagued with irregularities, lawsuits, protests, and bloodshed. As the Joe Biden campaign engaged in reclaiming a disputed election, a New State confederation was seeded as an informal alliance between East and West coast states. A definitive plan for secession was rolled out shortly thereafter by governors and other elected officials from so-called donor states — those contributing more tax money to the federal government than they receive. These states tended to be Democratically-led and were initially hit the hardest by Covid-19. For their part, Republican senators continually blocked federal financial bailouts for states and municipalities. Meanwhile multinational corporations were profiting from billions of stimulus tax dollars. The S&P 500 and Nasdaq indexes charted all-time highs. For many states a secession simply made economic sense.

With the help of the Supreme Court and the Attorney General, Trump declared his re-election at the close of 2020. In a concession speech Joe Biden echoed Al Gore from 2000, "for the sake of our unity as a people and the strength of our democracy, I offer my concession." Decades of incompetence finally broke the Democratic National Committee and progressives grabbed control from the moderates. A party coup would prime the secession.

While most of the secessionist planning took place via back-channel negotiations, a brazen media war was waged in support of the cause. After Trump's illegitimate claim to victory, secessionist leaders made no effort to conceal their intentions. They reasoned that the President and his circle would interpret the strategy as an appropriation of their own tactics — all hot air and bluster. In the first few months of 2021 the word "TREASON!!!" was included in Presidential tweets more than two dozen times, but no significant response was taken other than the threat of lawsuits.

New State independence was declared on April 15, 2021, following a coordinated effort by millions of residents and businesses based in the original 20 secessionist states to suspend payments to the U.S. federal government. The original states were: Maine, Vermont, Massachusetts, Rhode Island, Connecticut, New York, New Jersey, Pennsylvania, Maryland, Virginia, Michigan, Illinois, Minnesota, Colorado, New Mexico, Nevada, California, Oregon, Washington, and Hawaii. Shortly thereafter South Florida liberated itself to join the New State. The District of Columbia followed after sorting out a series of complications related to its status as a former national capital. In the end, the New State map closely followed boundaries established when states decided to expand Medicaid in the 2010s.

On that tax independence day, residents of the New State were told that they would be protected from the non-payment of federal tributes to the United States; a decree which went a long way towards quieting dissent in the countryside. Days of celebratory street manifestations were to follow. In the Soft Secession the scales of Federalism were tipped toward regionalism.

Hard boundaries were not raised immediately to mark New State territory. Migration was permitted and new citizens registered their affiliation with the New State through an online portal which was an early component in a vast network architecture that would be designed to provide access to basic government services. Claiming a New State identification number would immediately trigger the revocation of U.S. citizenship and furnish guaranteed monthly income payments.

The New State is not a country in the manner of a typical modern nation state. Governance is decentralized, local, and participatory. There is a President who is elected by ranked choice vote but she can only serve one four-year term with strictly limited executive powers. It was also decided through a plebiscite that the New State would retain its generic name, have no national flag, no anthem, and no police force, but it did need its own currency. An injection of new money would quantitatively ease the difficult challenge of coordinating and building out a social infrastructure. Inflation was a worry to be left for another time. Executing plans for a new government apparatus was a massive undertaking, particularly during an economic depression. But let's not get tangled in policy details, these are just sketches from a secession.

It is worth noting that the New State benefitted from serendipity. A vaccine to stop Covid-19 was discovered and approved by a group of researchers at Oxford University in May 2021. By June it was widely available. Having California in the New State was an immense benefit because of its advanced research and technology sectors. We can characterize the secession as "soft" because a vast majority of the military-industrial complex was absorbed in the break up. The revolution was bloodless and bureaucratic.

For some years the Pacific States, and California in particular, had been facing off against the federal government to maintain an adherence to stricter emissions and climate regulations. Reducing and capturing atmospheric carbon became a top priority for the New State under the direction of Californian policy makers. Parallels were frequently drawn between the Pacific secessionist block and the breakaway nation described in Ernest Callenbach's 1974 novel Ecotopia. In the book, the Pacific Northwest states (Washington and Oregon) join California in a bioregional movement that separates from the United States in 1980. Ecotopia contains various proposals that are unworkable in the New State, but it does offer useful sketches for a large-scale plan which is oriented towards an ecological

horizon — the only horizon that really matters in the end. It remains a popular title in the New State to this day. From an ecological standpoint, the most significant plan adopted by the New State was the Green New Deal. see also page 231

The political foundations for the New State assembled from unfulfilled promises gathered from the ill-fated campaigns of Bernie Sanders. His Democratic Socialists party helped to transform the New State from a version of Keynesianism to a multi-party social-democratic system. A guaranteed income, climate action, universal healthcare, and free college were adopted over time. Legislative priorities hewed closely to Sanders' 21st Century Economic Bill of Rights. His portrait is now on our digital currency.

In the first years of the New State there was massive economic and personal suffering. There was social unrest and real doubts about whether our statecraft would succeed. But as difficult as that period was, it created the conditions for artists to act politically alongside other workers towards a common cause. There were no means to build an individual practice; no market. The guaranteed income was just enough to get by. But what's slowly emerging is the framework to support creative work under the terms that we've long wished for.

A recounting of the fate of the United States will be left for another time.

Postscript: This text was first written in April 2020 and updated in August to account for the Black Lives Matters protests following the murder of George Floyd on May 25, 2020. It is now December 2020. Joe Biden has decisively defeated Donald Trump in the Popular and Electoral College vote counts, yet the threat of a secession continues, not from the left but from a large faction of Trump loyalists who refuse to recognize the election results. Once again, progressives in the United States will tie their political fates to the center; we will see how long it holds.

1 Sam Adler-Bell, "Coronavirus Has Given the Left a Historic Opportunity. Can They Seize It?," The Intercept, April 14, 2020, accessed April 26, 2020, https://theintercept.com

2 Jerry Saltz, "The Last Days of the Art World ... and Perhaps the First Days of a New One Life after the coronavirus will be very different." New York Magazine, April 2, 2020, accessed April 25, 2020, https://vulture.com

3 Magda Sawon, "This Is the Toughest Challenge My Business Has Ever Faced. But Here's Why Small Galleries Like Mine Will Come Out Alive," Artnet, April 27, 2020, accessed April 27, 2020, https://news.artnet.com

4 Dave Beech, Art and Postcapitalism: Aesthetic Labor, Automation and Value Production. (London: Pluto Books, 2019), 41.

2026

Yesterday, the High Desert State Prison in California was dismantled successfully. It had been closed in February this year together with nine other prisons in the United States. The closings are a consequence of the declining arrests of petty criminals, especially the ones being accused of dealing marihuana. To share her joy about the development, civil-rights activist Angela Davis held a speech in Harlem this morning, which was live-streamed by more than three million people worldwide.

2028

Today, the European Gaming Congress
held its first public conference in the Gardens
of Castell Gandolfo. The former summer
residency of the pope has officially been
handed over to the European Gaming
Congress by the Catholic Church and will
now be used as a center for research and
spatial experimentation.

2028

Today, US-American Rapper and Music Producer Shawn Corey Carter, known as Jay-Z, announced to leave his home in Bel-Air. The 30'000 square meter house will be provided as a residency and working space for young economical talents who cannot afford to rent a home in Los Angeles. Carter and his wife Beyoncé moved to France, as they are in the process of finding ways to open-source their champagne company Armand de Brignac.

Meghan Rolvien, *coding, changing, learning*

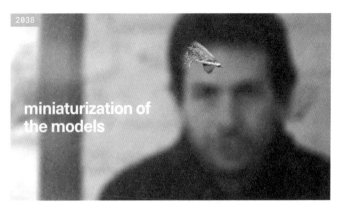

miniaturization of
the models

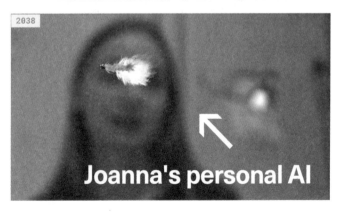

Joanna's personal AI

70

Audrey's personal AI

Jaromil's personal AI

And their personal AIs

2030

Today, a major step was made during the planetary negotiations in Ruanda. The Nile has officially been acknowledged having the status of a legal entity.

2030

Today, Joscha Bach, Vice President of Research at the AI Foundation, introduced a computer guided system for the allocation of staple foods during the planetary negotiations in Sanaa. The system was influenced by Cybersyn, a cybernetic model designed by Stafford Beer in 1971, which was aiming to develop a decentralized, cross-linked economy management for Chile, that could react dynamically based on a feedback model. The project was however cancelled after the military coup in 1973. Today, Bach was able to rewrite the system for countries troubled by famine. It will be tested in Yemen and Chad by the end of the year.

House of Statistics

Tirdad Zolghadr

2029

The House of Statistics was built in the sixties to amass the data of every East German citizen under the communist government. And when the wall came down, the idea was to demolish it as part of the so-called Kollhoff Plan, which was an attempt to Manhattanize the Alexanderplatz, through high rises and a nice fancy skyline. The House of Statistics was empty for about 10 years, before a group of artists called Abba, Allianz bedrohter Berliner Atelierhäuser, did a kind of intervention.

They forged a banner, a municipal city of Berlin official banner, saying that the House of Statistics would not be demolished. It would be devoted to cultural and social needs of the city of Berlin. And people believed in it just long enough. Even the cops believed in it, just long enough. The decision makers had to take a position on it. It's funny what a circus it was back in 2015, when the demolition of the House of Statistics was prevented. Nowadays, it's pretty banal that cities don't sell off public land for condominiums. You don't pit the cultural sector against city bureaucracy, against social facilities. You look for synergies. You allow for bottom-up participation in the planning process. Today, these things are pretty much obvious and not even worth a minor squabble in some Kreuzberg bar room. It's just what you do.

Back then, it was decided that the House of Statistics would not only be preserved, and renovated, but the volume would be doubled. More than doubled, to a hundred thousand square meters. So, it's quite a unique poly-functional experiment that was happening here. It's also something of a fairy tale ending for this crazy artistic intervention, and artistic agency in the name of the common good. In those days, it was a huge deal. The fact that artists managed to save the House of Statistics from demolition, and the fact that it became a success. During this transitional period, all kinds of cultural initiatives were using the house, temporarily, to do their thing, but also to create facts on the ground. To put this thing in the public eye, and to make sure that you can't just walk away from it politically. To make it a promise that's difficult to break.

Statista was a collaboration between KW and the ZKU. We pieced together about 10, 12 different playing fields that were all supporting the House of Statistics in one way or another. The fact that by some miracle the mayor, the technocrats, the cultural workers, the social workers, the tenants, were all more or less happy, led to this becoming a kind of blueprint. Thus, similar models were pursued elsewhere, all the way from the U.S to Tehran. Even in Bavaria they set up very similar templates in 2031. And as the German adage has it, if it works in Bavaria, it can work everywhere.

2019-2029, *Haus der Statistik*

2031

Today, Mila Keita was elected minister of agriculture in London. The Austrian-Senegalese politician is trained as an architect and has been campaigning for the promotion of drone-operated vertical farming during the last months. Her ministry was chosen by the quadratic voting principle that was tested in England for the first time. Amongst the voters, farmers and retired persons had set the highest preference degrees for the election.

Time-Machine Architectonics

Suhail Malik

On the occasion of the Venice Architecture Biennale 2038 press conference at ExRotaPrint, the political econoplexist calls in from 2031.

With the convergence of environmental and financial breakdowns in 2023 we reached the point at which everyone understood that there was nothing left to protect from the previous system.

This historic event has by now come to be commonly known as The Jackpot — a term adopted from William Gibson's novels of the 2010s onwards, in which it designates an undefined calamity in social relations and social condition. Just as long ago Gibson's coining of the term 'cyberspace' was quickly adopted to signify the commonplace of internet immersion, The Jackpot was a handy term to capture the total failure of the previous order eight years ago. We called it that because the breakdown wasn't due to the disappearance of wealth but the hyper-accumulation of most of the planet's capital by a very, very small number of people — the famous "1%" or 0.01%, a micro fraction of the planet's population. They won the lottery again and again, accumulating from even the greatest disasters by betting for them: Jackpot. For everyone and everything else — planetary systems, environmental mechanisms, and the rest of it — it was a calamity.

The lesson from '23 was that the basis for this kind of accumulation had to change. That premise was private property as it was enforced through the long history of sovereign authorities of the nation state formations in the North Atlantic, then more recently implemented across the planet by transnational alliances, contracts and agreements across nation states. As you already know in 2020, that system went further and further even after the warning of the 2008 Crash. It was a complete market failure in the sense that the markets totally failed, incapable of allocating resources with any degree of competence. The Jackpot.

So, by now, in 2031, private property is manifestly and commonly understood to no longer be a viable condition to keep things going — both for the human social system and also for the environment. It was already clear even by the first decade of his century that the environmental system was unable to maintain itself because of the consequences of the privatization of wealth and property accumulation.

But one of the political and theoretical struggles we have right now is that we don't know what the basis for social condition instead of liberalism should be. What is the social and political formation that does not have private property as its premise? There are many arguments about what to do based on two negative criteria: first, that private property cannot continue as the basis of a social system and, second, that communism is still untenable. At this point in time, we are still trying out many different systems and there are many different experiments to find out what to do after liberalism and neoliberalism.

There are some theoretical answers, there are some practical answers. Maybe the hardest problem is that the premises for most of these local and situated practices or theories oblige us to establish particular bounded claims and actions — for example, if the acting agency is taken to be an embodied individual, never mind a community, a firm, a specific organization, or a country; such formats assume enclosures and separations. And that assumption quickly leads to the requirement of enforceable private spaces which quickly seems to regress back to some variant of liberalism.

We've however come to appreciate that actions and systems need to be instead configured in terms of managed environments. That means both managing the environment but also being managed by the environment. This in turn requires a recursive feedback: that is, a responsive to and fro of what has just happened between any system and its environment, between what is internal to a system and what is external to it.

In this specific sense, recursion means that the system's output, which is in the future of the system's operation, will itself shape the future of the system. As a consequence, the concept of a masterplan, or of a final answer or solution, just isn't tenable anymore. Now, it's more about the dynamic organization and processes by which we get to maintain sustainable environments and provide viable conditions into the future.

In architecture, for example, the imperative to build a future now means that architectural forms are no longer about separating our private spaces from other spaces. If the wall, the roof or the floor were once viewed as a kind of separating or striating mechanism, these elements are now understood more as membranes or interfaces between an inside and an outside. Each involves a regulated transmission, leading in turn to an architecture directed by porosity rather than separation.

An architecture that adapts to the consequences of outcomes and their feedback into the construction schemes generates new results that can't be preplanned and are instead unpredictable. So, part of the post-Jackpot paradigm is that architects don't just build in space. They also build in time: stated as an imperative, what needs to be built are various time configurations. In this sense, and exemplarily, architecture now builds time-machines.

But, as said, intrinsic to this time construction is also that the unpredictability of the outputs is part of the future configured by the system dynamics. The characteristic uncertainty of the future of the system and the consequences of its output is what feeds back into the system itself. So, recursion is a speculative mechanism for promoting uncertainty and risk. In fact, we now assume that all systems processing risk are time-machines of this kind.

Of course, the processes and systems by which those inputs and outputs are organized also need to be regulated so that the unpredictability does not entail toxic outcomes. The contribution to larger environments, but also how they feed into other systems need to be managed. Again, architecture — or, more precisely, time-machine architectonics — has become a promising practice for thinking about such speculative organization.

What then are the viable parameters for such a speculative recursive architecture? What risks does it involve? How are these to be mitigated? After the multiple convergent crises of 2023, we finally understood that there are no more externalities. That there never had been. In a way, planetary integration — which was realized in part by the risk-promoting financial system necessary to The Jackpot, and in part by environmental breakdown — definitively means that there is nowhere else to deposit the exhaust. We've come to appreciate that a system's waste is itself a component of its speculative organization. We have just the planet itself, and the residues of the processes feedback directly into it.

So, one of the most significant shifts post-Jackpot is the increased responsiveness to how disparate systemic operations aggregate into an overall system which shouldn't produce or amplify toxic speculation — toxic with regard to both the distribution of wealth or capital, and also to the environmental consequences. see also page 181 Regulatory mechanisms are really significant to avoid the reflux of a system's exhaust into its speculative organization.

What has obviously been needed — even before '23 — is a framework that protects common interests from both private and state interests. The construction of such framework exceeds nation state authorities but doesn't presume a planetary state, which just upscales the problem. Some model of a distributed, yet common legal framework seems the most promising as we're still trying to construct the new post-Jackpot era. We are now working towards a binding legal framework for everyone and everything that is distributed (so it can be locally organized) while being nested within a larger regulatory framework (because we don't permit ourselves the alibi of cost-free externalities).

The binding legal framework needs to be distributed, multilayered, local, yet combinable within a planetary scheme. see also page 161 We know that it can be anything that we want it to be, but what still needs to be understood is how to fabricate a recursive organization that's protective — and that's another problem for the architecture of speculative organisation.

Suhail Malik & Joanna Pope, *The Property Drama, again*

Suhail Malik, *(eco)sytemic*

Some Notes on the Term Jackpot

Michael Stoeppler

Looming large after 2023. Prompted in reading William Gibson, **THE PERIPHERAL,** Penguin, London 2014

In Chapter 12. THYLACINE a conversation (*set in italics*) in bed takes place, where the term *jackpot* is mentioned for the first time in the novel. *"Before the jackpot. ... You can't go there. Nobody can. But information can be exchanged, so money can be made there."* P. 38 The money making motive is essential, as outlined in detail in chapter 20. POLT (Polt, of course). 37 pages further, the Peripheral plot problem of transferring money into the past is pondered, via winning" in their state's next lottery. The payment would be entirely legitimate." P.75 For now we are at p. 39, still in italics conversational style, where the first jackpot time frame is mentioned: *"How far back can they go?" "Twenty twenty-three, earliest. He thinks something changed, then; reached a certain level of complexity. Something nobody there had any reason to notice."* In the next paragraph, same chapter, now normal type, narrative mode, the jackpot is placed in a second time frame of "...midcentury, just as the jackpot really got going." Where midcentury refers to the Twenty First Century. Let's jump to Chapter 79. THE JACKPOT for details. "And first of all that it was no one's thing. That it was multicausal, with no particular beginning and no end. More a climate than an event, so not the way apocalypse stories liked to have a big event ..." P. 319 "It was androgenic... . Not that they'd known what they were doing, had meant to make problems, but they'd caused it anyway ... systemic, multiplex, seriously..., over about forty years. ... The assemblers, nanobots, had come later ... cared for it all, constantly in this time after the jackpot ... for them it was more about other species, the other great dying, ... diseases that were never quite the one big pandemic but big enough to be historic events ... science ... had been the wild card, the twist..." P. 321 Let's keep in mind that the motive of **no particular beginning and no end** strongly resonates with Stafford Beer, Heart of Enterprise. The "planning loops ... do not stop or start". STAFFORD BEER, ... AND PLANS, IN: THE HEART OF ENTERPRISE. COMPANION VOLUME TO BRAIN OF THE FIRM. 1979 P. 342. Readers are asked to keep in mind that "there is no beginning and no end, no superior and no inferior authority" in planning. P. 350 "Planing is not an activity resulting in products called plans: it is a continuous process, whereby the process itself — namely that of aborting the plans — is the pay-off. The plans do not have to be implemented by those in authority: what the authority does, constitutes the plan — and its realization." P. 338 The second motive in Gibson that resonates strongly with Beer is that of **breaking the time barrier.** "Suppose that we can acquire data about stability that can be transformed into information (which changes us) about the possibility, the likelihood, of *incipient* instability: then, and only then, do we have a chance to avert it. ... if we have real time data and if we use them to measure the likelihood of instability, instead of trying to impute necessary results from an unsound theory of causality, then we have the opportunity to brake the time barrier. Action may be taken now, in order that incipient instability shall not become actual." STAFFORD BEER, CALM AND ALARM, EBD. P. 376/77 Taking **action without particular beginning and no end** — which is key to **breaking the time barrier** — "is not a matter of COUNTING possible states, but of MATCHING them." STAFFORD BEER, THE EXIT, EBD. P. 89 The task facing us is to figure out architectonics of "total plasticity or possibility", as Suhail Malik see also page 83 aptly termed it in 2031, "what needs to be built are various time configurations." Planning and running us in/to The New Serenity, architecting 2038 took Tense Logic and Modal Logic rather than mere computational crunching of behemothical Data Sets, Statistics and Theories of Probability. "These things cannot be forced." STAFFORD BEER, DESIGNING FREEDOM (1973), P.43 Finding a way out without using force turned out to be key to The New Serenity. Radical forcelessness — not to be confused with powerlessness — helped turning mere transition into real change. In prospect of breaking the time barrier towards The New Serenity, personalities under deconstruction left us with faltering traits of error, turbidity, opinion, striving, arbitrariness and transcience. "Next we come to Sir John. (Who) has been largely automated. His ego is huge, and his personality is stamped on everyone's television screen. He looks like the last word in free-ranging variety. But all this is illusory. Much of the variety he handles as input, as we met him, has been processed by machines, in the cause of reducing its variety. He himself, as we met him, has been processed by machines". STAFFORD BEER, THE EXIT, EBD. P.91 "Investment in persona. ... The monetization... ." WILLIAM GIBSON, 119. SIR HENRY, EBD. P.468 Abandoning the Sir thing helped us aborting personalized power-structures which led to "a major devolution of power". STAFFORD BEER, THE FUTURE THAT CAN BE DEMANDED NOW, IN: DESIGNING FREEDOM, P.34 Charisma doesn't take a chance with us in 2038. Naive? Of course. Nothing new happens between people without naivete. "Not about profit so much as keeping fresh sources of novelty." WILLIAM GIBSON, 85. FUTURE PEOPLE, EBD. P.349

"And there is none left to say a loud NO to that — until the people themselves say No." STAFFORD BEER, THE FUTURE THAT CAN BE DEMANDED NOW, IN: DESIGNING FREEDOM, P. 33 The change from NO to No is a giant leap for a single person, a small step for the people. "Because people who couldn't imagine themselves capable of evil were at a major disadvantage in dealing with people who didn't need to imagine, because they already were". WILLIAM GIBSON, 123. COMPOUND, EBD. P. 481 Were. Already. Indeed. Not us. Not anymore. Never again. Never ever. Relax.

In the mid 20s of the 21st Century, when the jackpot started to kick in, the domination of people who *didn't need to imagine* themselves capable of evil, the sovereignity of the resident, dwelling, inward oriented populations of the planet shifted towards a domination of people who *couldn't imagine* themselves capable of evil, leading towards a transient, outward oriented way of living together in a viable system without any need for sovereignity at all. Now and again the once silent find a voice in their "journey towards liberty". PLATO, *THE LAWS* 701C The kick-in of the jackpot in the mid 20s marked another of the rare occasions of this event. Though instead of leading to a "sovereignity of the audience", so aptly termed "theatocracy" EBD. 700 A-D more than 2000 years ago, the people who couldn't imagine themselves capable of evil were determined to come up with a new, naive way of living together. Finding a voice they came up with three neologisms to express a love for their time. They called their form of domination *Architectocracy*, their geological time *Architectozean* and their form of governance *Architectonomy*. The sources render their condition by the early 30s as tripleA living, an already outdated concept of assessment in bloated technical terms, a habit that happened to get dropped entirely by the late 30s in favour of a much more elegant, archi-tectonic notion: The New Serenity.

Francesca Bria, *Surfin'1*

Mara Balestrini, *orchestrated (eco)systems*

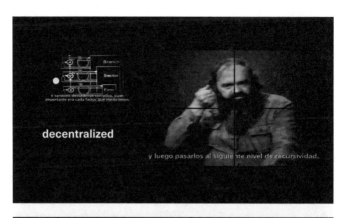

Stafford Beer, *complexity*

2032

Last night, Keller Easterling was elected the next president of the United States of America. The architect and activist managed to win the race with 72% of the votes and thereby out-rivaled her fellow campaigners Tulsi Gabbard and Jacques Berman Webster. The election battle proceeded peaceful and festive. Easterling's first appearance as president was characterized by her two-hours speech which appeared as an optimistic message to all the people of the world.

After the Attention Economy:
Notes toward a cosmo-financial
New Serenity

Erik Bordeleau

"Like a tropical storm,
I, too, may one day become 'better organized'."

Lydia Davis

1

Our ways of making sense of ourselves and the world had been irremediably transformed by the advent of web 2.0 technologies at the turn of the 21st century. Our social media were (and of course still are) more than mere means of communication: they are constitutive of the relational fabric of our lives. Their infrastructure is our subjective intra-structure. There is no clear distinction between an objective, techno-digital outside and a subjective, intimate inside. Human beings had become media mutants, want it or not. *There is a private life of feelings, but not for us.* We had to come to terms with the fact that, as Thomas Lamarre had suggested in his analysis of the late 1990s' Pokemon incident,[1] we could only learn to navigate this fully integrated, vortex-like attentional field if we accepted our condition as *self-intoxicating media subjects.* This was the only way we could start reverse imagineering capitalist sorcery.

2

For most of the 20s, the business model of the internet was still predicated on a mix of data predation and organized distraction. How could we force corporations to open up the algorithmic black boxes that governed the attention economy? How could social network platforms be turned into thriving p2p digital commons? *What if, in short, social media belonged to its users?* Social media architectures were designed to keep us captive, fully leveraging the network effect and its addictive social validation feedback loops.

Welcome to the social media abyss. What one wouldn't do for the promise of a never-ending series of digitally-induced dopamine hits? We had all heard stories of Silicon Valley workers actively limiting their children's exposure to screens and disconnecting themselves from the very platforms they had contributed in creating. Or how more and more people were going on digital detox retreats, in order to steer themselves away from a state of continuous partial attention and relieve their online anxiety symptoms.

Something more had to be done in order to rewire our collective digitally distributed soul, our post-industrial general intellect. The collected data we generated through our platformized interactions were aggregated and later traded on behavioral future markets. This process defined the regime that Shoshana Zuboff described as surveillance capitalism. Data was the new oil. The new Capital. Das Digital! Some data-driven markets optimists were calling for a New Deal on Data, a progressive data-sharing mandate to address the monopoly ownership over Big Data and force data sharing to other startups and public actors.[2] This reformist stance was interesting, although it simply displaced the extractivist practice and didn't address the problem that a lot of the data being collected shouldn't exist in the first place.

3

If we were to reclaim our social media and fully consider them as designable living (and intoxicating) milieus, we needed to operate a paradigm shift from an attention economy running on addiction to *co-immunizing, cosmo-financial ecologies of attention*. This wasn't an easy task.

The attention economy monetized the attention of individuals; the attentional field was financialized through and through. The value never resided in the individual, but in the relationscape. That much we knew. But the conversion formulas between the realm of the attentional and the realm of the financial still remained fairly obscure. How would an attentional flow turn into a financial flow? Was it, as Stalin allegedly intuited in a moment of massifying lucidity, that quantity had a quality all of its own?

A late cyber-vitalist prophet of late 20th century had contributed in no small measure to a new understanding of collective metastability, bringing to the fore the anthropological notion of the dividual in an attempt to reinterpret the passage to a floating exchange rate regime initiated by the Nixon administration back in the early 1970s. [3] The positive unconscious of never-been-modern societies was encrypted in cursive and recursive financial signs that spoke of options, spreads and implied volatility. Few were in grade of deciphering them; in fact, most people felt a sincere aversion toward finance's modes of abstraction.

4

Money had always been the master's fiction of last resort. In his book about economy addressed to his daughter back in 2017, the ex-Greece minister of finance Yannis Varoufakis had an interesting way of describing the mechanism of money issuance and its strangely qualified relation to futurity. Bankers, he explains, were the only people, back then, authorized to travel in the future to bring back monetary units into the present. In order to meaningfully engage in the design of alternative socio-political configurations

Feuchtigkeit": 99.9, "Brutnest-Temperatur": 27.7, "Spannung": 4.03}
hiveeyes/open-hive-hermann/default/1/data.json {"time": "2019/12/29 16:09:07", "Gewicht": 0.472,
"Aussen-Temperatur": 21.4, "Aussen-Feuchtigkeit": 26.2, "Innen-Temperatur": 21.5, "Innen-
Feuchtigkeit": 55.3, "Batterie-Spannung": 3.98}hiveeyes/c366... 1b3-97aa-66f63127471b/
spielwiese/node-1/data.json
{"weight1":37488,"weight2":44451,"temp1":0.06,"temp2":0.00, temp... humwww": 65"}hive
yes/27041c2a-8afd-4a1e-b3ae-44233fa1f06b/mois/yun/data.json {"temperature hive1": 19.2, "weight
hive2": 25.0, "weight hive1": 30.0, "humidity hive2": 82.2, "humidity hive1": 92.8, "brightness":
10.0, "temperature hive2": 19.0, "geobash": "u33d9", "temperature outside": 21.0, "temperature
inside": 18.2}hiveeyes/01CQPYC57PYFMX81CDXND92CD5/Balkon/Stand/data.json {"Uptime_min": 7543,
"IP": "192.168.1.10", "Temperatur": 17.5, "Luftfeuc... e": 45.0999924741 29 "Taupunkt":
5.479912203731...   Gew... t":
0.16689689619   990..,
hiveeyes/01CQ...57...1C... CD5 all...ut...son...   4...552...}hiveeyes/
666/garten/beute...s/data...json__"havec... ... payload_loads: { temperature 1.3, \
"temperature_3\": 0.6, \"analog_is_1\": 46..., "analog_in 2\": 46.41, \"analo... 3\": 3.99, \
"relative_humidity_2\": 66.5), \"payload_raw\": \"AQISQQICE1ECEwANAmi9B2cABgHCAT8=\", \
"hardware_serial\": \"00465D1CCFB4A17A\", \"port\": 1.0, \"metadata\": {\"location_source\": \
"registry\", \"data_rate\": \"SF7BW125\", \"modulation\": \"LORA\", \"longitude\": 13.07855, \
"coding_rate\": \"4/5\", \"frequency\": 868.1, \"gateways\": [{\"location_source\": \"registry\",
\"gtw_id\": \"eui-b827ebfffe3eelab\", \"timestamp\": 764359859, \"altitude\": 5, \"longitude\":
13.078521, \"rf_chain\": 1, \"snr\": 11, \"time\": \"2019-12-29T15:06:53.812773Z\", \"latitude\":
52.38949, \"rssi\": -75, \"channel\": 0}], \"time\": \"2019-12-29T15:06:53.8331409182\", \\
"latitude\": 52.38961}}\" from topic \"hiveeyes/testdrive/ttn/be-one/data.json\"."]

complexity

2038

We had the idea to empower people with cryptog

2029

and to re-think value at the end of the economy as we know it, we had to, somehow paradoxically, learn to engage more closely, more technically, more creatively, with the speculative power of finance. The financial class certainly didn't have the monopoly on risk-generating and risk-hedging practices. How we leverage our own capacities to take risks and enter into metastable collective compositions, beyond what is deemed "possible" — or insurable? —, was to become a decisive element of any successful post-capitalist politics to come.

5

In the late 2010s, the advent of distributed ledger technologies (blockchain) had triggered an age of experiment in online collective formation, a sort of cooperative renaissance of the web for the exploration of new ways to achieve consensus in digital ecosystems. A new generation of artists was getting involved in the blockchain space and was generating companies and other cooperative endeavors with an artistic toolset. The distinction between digital communities and the organization of value capture — and exposure — became increasingly blurry. The word community rapidly became the new darling of venture capitalists, as many were speculating around the emergence of paid community social network. Art was ambiguously signaling both the generative informality of social life, and the process of discovering new ways of formalizing sociality. What were the different techno-social components defining these new organizational forms that combine the immutability of a shared past with the programmability of a freely commonized future? Were we finally, albeit shadily and "pharmacologically", moving toward the "organized networks" or "networks with consequences" Lovink and

Rossiter had called for? The hope was that blockchain technologies, through cryptographic consensus, could provide a technical solution to the problem of trust and cooperation in large-scale digital collectives. In a world moving toward accrued social fragmentation, the way we create new techno-social modes of coordination had indeed become crucial. As Yves Citton pointed out in his seminal *Toward an Ecology of Attention*, the real challenge was to terraform new metamorphic passages between the micro scale of collective presence and the macro scale of media aggregations. [4] [Fig. 1]

6

Economies are assembled from different types of flows, that is, incorporated values made liquid. To register and manifest these flows, we use what we call *currencies*. What if the solution for wiring our economies anew was to break-down the capitalist mono-economy into a myriad of living cryptocurrencies coordinating socio-financial flows and networks in new ways? As Joichi Ito, director of the MIT Media Lab, suggested in 2018 in *Resisting Reduction: A Manifesto*,

"We live in a civilization in which the primary currencies are money and power — where more often than not, the goal is to accumulate both at the expense of society at large. This is a very simple and fragile system compared to the Earth's ecosystems, where myriads of "currencies" are exchanged among processes to create hugely complex systems of inputs and outputs with feedback systems that adapt and regulate stocks, flows, and connections. (…) The paradigm of a single master currency has driven many corporations and institutions to lose sight of their original missions." [5]

104

The Plant, *complexity*

Denis Roio, *Data vs. Space*

Erik Bordeleau, *World Game*

Fig. 1: Cryptocommunists of the world, unite! Blockchain means you can collectively own your means of relation.

loops, *coexist*

Francesca Bria, *Data vs. Space*

The key point here is that we needed to conceive of money not just as an external economic factor synonym with value extraction, dispossession and toxic accumulation, but *as a configurative power that shapes our attentional milieus*. The possibility offered by blockchain to multiply monetary self-issuance appeared as a way to renew our collective incorporations, the way we come together without becoming one, generating derivative value along the way. This utopia was alive and well in the early days of the crypto-space: a myriad of self-issuances that could be modulated at will, following the affordances of a given ecosystem and in response to the inter-species web of entanglements in which they are embedded.[6]

7

"The economy is the precarious art of snatching emergent order out of affect." Brian Massumi, The Power at the End of the Economy.

8

Blockchains or distributed ledger technologies are most often associated with cryptocurrencies. But it is perhaps more interesting to conceive of them first as *constitutional or institutional* orders: a set of protocols by which individuals, firms or algorithms, can make economic and political exchanges. see also page 175 In this sense, blockchains look a lot like jurisdictions, or virtual "countries" (hence the famous rallying cry of blockchain's anarcho-capitalist's early days, "code is law"). And just like countries, blockchains have systems of governance, usually open source protocols which define how individuals interact and transact with one another. Whether we are talking about Bitcoin, Ethereum, or other blockchain ecosystems, the big idea is roughly the

The Dymaxion Map was invented by Buckminster Fuller

The map's initial purpose was to be used as a giant board for Fuller's "World Game"

Buckminster Fuller, *World Game*

see also page 118

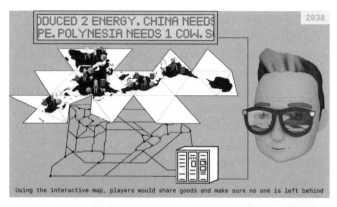

Using the interactive map, players would share goods and make sure no one is left behind

Buckminster Fuller, *World Game*

Cédric Libert and Buckminster Fuller, or*chestrated (eco)systems*

same: governance markets are created to award coins to those who enforce the governance rules of a given protocol for interaction. The design of incentives thus becomes integral to consensus-driven technical systems. Blockchains create a medium for people to be rewarded for enforcing decentralized governance at scale. In short, blockchains are governance-making machines — see also page 123 the protocol is the institution. And as such, they allow for the formation of all sorts of digital membranes, economic enclosures, and eventually, new commons 3.0.

What is at stake then, from a crypto-financial point of view, is the process of incorporation of forms-of-value as such, i.e.: the legal or digital codification whereby an economic asset is enclosed, securitized, monetized, that is, *contingentialized*. An economy founded on a blockchain makes it possible to issue tokens in which various governance and property rights, various pre-established circulation and transmission rules would be programmed — a new form of network-based value. These techno-social formations or legal and digital incorporations constitute what Economic Space Agency (ECSA) calls "economic spaces," meaning spaces within which it is the very organization of our ways of "risking and speculating together" that becomes the main vector of valorization.[7]

9

Many anarcho-monadologists and other new materialists argued that commons weren't so much about new social constitutions, but rather new lived geographies, locally grounded and transversally felt. They made clear that engaging with the enabling constraints of derivative finance and cryptoeconomics was risky and potentially problematic.

Abstracting or not abstracting the commons? That was the question. At best, cryptoeconomics could act as a neganthropic *pharmakon* (as Bernard Stiegler put it): a perspective in which the economy itself works as a *general therapy for the biosphere*, reversing the destructive course of the Anthropocene by favoring the always localized slowing down of entropic processes.[8] At worse, the proliferation of cryptoeconomics' modes of organization might actually signify the destruction—i.e. the economic reduction—of countless other types of worlding practices, more subtle, more improbable, less calculable, too. The quest for scalability, Anna Tsing reminds us, tends to banish meaningful diversity, that is, diversity that might make a difference. Indeed, just as more traditional capitalist formations, cryptoeconomically-enabled modes of governance might be predating upon forms of transindividual sociality that have been, as Fred Moten and Stefano Harney have explained in *The Undercommons* (2013), militantly preserved away from for-profit capitalist computability. In this regard, the whole *New Serenity* world contract architecture has been designed in strict concordance with *the principle of non-scalability*.[9] Yet, up to this day, some critics sustain that the main achievement resulting from the establishment in 2031 of a blockchain-based radical bureaucracy was the reinforcement of governance as "the extension of whiteness on a global scale". The fact that one of the guiding principles of this mutant bureaucracy was the anarcho–nihilist *leitmotif* "We are nothing and so can you" wasn't the least of ironies.

10

By facilitating the creation of scalable programmable organizations, cryptoeconomics re-opens the debate around economic planning and performance measurement. There is no economy (Stafford Beer had been very clear about this point) without its own set of econometrics to identify and quantify the causal relationships between economic phenomena. But how to measure what economists have traditionally called "intangible assets" — something that corporate accounting as always struggled to account for — outside or beyond the traditional means of the market? The question of economic valuation is a delicate one because (surplus) value measurements happen to be highly performative, that is: they tend to modify the very values they were meant to know at a distance. Or to paraphrase Donna Haraway's provocative and staying-with-the-trouble insight: it matters what worlds world worlds; and *it matters what measures measure measures.*

see also page 181

11

In *The Power at the End of the Economy*, Brian Massumi suggests that "nothing divides and multiplies the individual so much as its own relation to the future".[10] The question of how we expose ourselves to the unforeseeable, or how we allow the ecstatic requirements of futurity to seep through the present, is central to any discussion regarding collective self-organization. It points to the way we conceive of our common power, our differential sense of shared potentiality as we search for ways of subtracting ourselves from the self-valorization imperative governing our lives. Beyond the mere consensus on shared data, what kind of techno-social recursions — collective rituals, *proofs-of-celebration* and other metamorphic procedures of *belonging-in-becoming* — could we imagine for the infra-state disjunctive collectives and other transnational digital tribes to come? How could we bring about new calibrations between the realm of the quantitative and qualitative aspects of living, allowing for a wider range of values and life nurturing practices to gain currency?

12

Cosmopolitics is concerned with more-than-human communities and the way they attune with their associated milieus. The cosmofinancial proposal extends this view by integrating the promises and challenges raised by cryptoeconomics and derivative finance's affordances. *The cosmofinancial art of belonging in becoming foregrounds value discovery processes that are not confined to the logic of the market.* For what we owe to one another is not something in particular: it is the very unknown that envelops our existences, the zones of opacity and indetermination delineated by our more or less felicitous encounters. The cosmo—in cosmo–politics/technics/finance refers to the unknown constituted by these multiple, divergent worlds and to the articulations of which they are capable of. Many of these articulations aren't readily available. Virtual values tend to resist usual modes of categorization. The other as expression of a possible world is always in danger of being generalized, explained away and managed out. Everyone knows how stifling it can be when one is asked to list or enumerate "their values"—for organizational purpose, political correctness or otherwise. Values exist entangled, in relation. They require the patient elaboration of an ecology of fluctuating practices to find their way to expression. They require a welcoming culture of the interstices where burgeoning aspirations and historically-embedded, often tacit practices can resonate with one another and reveal themselves transindividually. Tellingly, when she tries to characterize this atmospheric mode of contagion, the great cosmopolitical thinker Isabelle Stengers refers to the delicate interstices where dreams meet each other: "Only whom who dreams can accept the modification of its dream. Only dreams or fabulations, because they are enjoyments of living values, can greet the interstices without the panic effect of who is afraid of losing grip."[11]

13

We had to learn all over again that what is valuable in our practices is also what is most vulnerable: vulnerable to the standardizing mystique of management, vulnerable to the extractive regime of generalized equivalence — vulnerable to the generalizing pretenses of governance. The cosmo-financial proposal was set to continuously explore the heterogeneous expressions and (in)formalizations of our mutual indebtedness, in order to foster differential collective incorporations that resisted the flattening of social, cultural and ecological values.

Ultimately, the rethinking of financial processes of value measurement as worlding practice gestured towards a shift from the neoliberal subject of interest to the protean figures of the futurial conservationist, the radical commonist, and the transindividual metastable ensemble.

15

感 / gǎn: to feel to move to touch to affect feeling emotion; Gǎn conveys a sense of contagion.
Gǎn mao: a cold; Gǎn xing: sexual excitement.

官 / guǎn: government official / organ of the body

感官 / gǎn guǎn: sense organ

1 In December 1997, after an episode of Pokémon was aired on Japanese TV, tens of thousands of children reportedly experienced seizures, a phenomenon dubbed the "Pokemon shock." For Lamarre, this incident provides an insight into the specific parameters for what he calls "the attention-reason complex of broadcast television", where attention works as a dark precursor amidst different procedures of segmentation generating different types of flows. Anime Ecology, University of Minnesota Press, 2018.

2 Viktor Mayer-Schönberger and Thomas Ramge, Reinventing Capitalism in the Age of Big Data, New York, 2018.

3 "We no longer find ourselves dealing with the mass/individual pair. Individuals have become "dividuals," and masses, samples, data, markets, or "banks." Perhaps it is money that expresses the distinction between the two societies best, since discipline always referred back to minted money that locks gold as numerical standard, while control relates to floating rates of exchange, modulated according to a rate established by a set of standard currencies." Gilles Deleuze, "Postscript on Control Societies", Negotiations, Columbia University Press, 1995, p.180.

4 Yves Citton, The Ecology of Attention, Trans. by Barnaby Norman,: Polity Press, Malden and Cambridge, 2017.

5 Joichi Ito, Resisting Reduction: A Manifesto, 2018. https://jods.mitpress.mit.edu/pub/resisting-reduction

6 For more details about this pluralist and anarchiving understanding of cryptoeconomics, see Economic Space Agency, "On Intensive Self-Issuance", in Inte Gloerich, Geert Lovink and Patricia de Vries (eds.), MoneyLab Reader 2: Overcoming the Hype, Amsterdam: Institute of Network Cultures, p.232-242.

7 Dick Bryan, Benjamin Lee, Akseli Virtanen and Robert Woznitzer, "Economics back into Cryptoeconomics," Medium (September 11, 2018), https://medium.com/econaut/economics-back-to-cryptoeconomics-20471f5ceeea

8 Bernard Stiegler, The Neganthropocene, Open Humanity Press, 2018.

9 Anna Tsing, "On Nonscalability: The Living World Is Not Amenable to Precision-Nested Scales", Common Knowledge, 18 (3), 2012, p.505–524.

10 Duke University Press, Durham, 2015, p. 9.

11 Isabelle Stengers, Penser avec Whitehead, Édition Seuil, Paris, 2002, p. 570 (my translation)

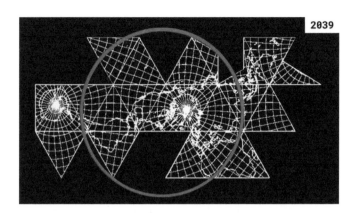

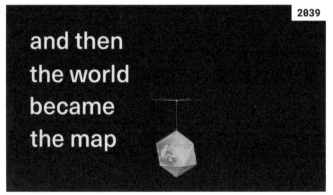

and then
the world
became
the map

Diann Bauer, *post(s)*

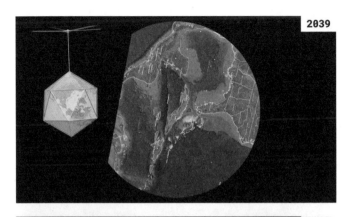

2039

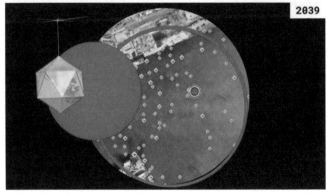

2039

see also page 110

119

2035

Today, US-American service company Uber has officially been registered as a working cooperation. The company had been criticized for its exploitation of drivers since many years. They were pressurized due to the rating systems and the lack of working insurance. Former attempts to build unions between drivers have been fended off by Uber through specific strategies preventing communication. During last month, employees of Uber have managed to team up and develop an alternative business model. A cooperatively owned network of drivers is now able to set up the payment rates and working rules democratically and transparently.

Beecoin

Tirdad Zolghadr

Behind the door it said "careful, bees". The project started as a collaboration between a number of different collectives. Nascent, which is invested in crypto technologies, More Bees, which is a collective of artists and beekeepers, Hive Eyes, which was interested in accumulating data on bees through different sensors, and the Kunstrepublik Collective, which is essentially the Zentrum für Kunst und Urbanistik. The core was five different beehives, the flagship of Beecoin. Since then it has been growing into a kind of holdings or stock company devoted to the common good as opposed to profit.

More precisely, it's devoted to the wellbeing of bees. More and more member joined the organization by building up a hive on their own and monitoring their bees with our sensors. If your bees are thriving, you are partaking in the value chain, you can accumulate the currency which we have issued and take an active part in the decision-making processes of the Beecoin project. And just as the House of Statistics became something of a success story, so did the Beecoin project. The fact that the wellbeing of bees is the actual cornerstone of the whole biosphere in Europe and elsewhere became common knowledge in the early 2020s. And Beecoin turned into a powerhouse in terms of lobbying for bees' interests. The cryptocurrency offered ways to regulate the participation while it maintained the system of equal votes. The network of participants grew broader and the scope turned planetary. Beecoin accumulated colossal resources, which were then redistributed into everything from political agitation to perfecting beehive and bee-monitoring technologies, and also aiding progressive ecologically smart farmers in their political struggles. It kind of worked. And it's a scary machine now.

Tirdad Zolghadr, 2019, *beecoins*

2029

The beecoin Project

"...the beecoin project expanded the notion of common property as the reproduction of a species we depend on daily to uphold our ecosystems – bees..."

Tirdad Zolghadr, 2029, *beecoins*
beehive, 2029, *beecoins*

2035

Today, the ICC Building in Berlin has reopened after 21 years of standstill. Its closing in 2014 was a consequence of enormous operating costs. The concept for reuse of the former International Congress Center had been decided by a gaming process seven years ago. In a Massively Multiplayer Online Game launched in 2027, participants were testing competing spatial and programmatical proposals for the building. After 6 months of gaming, the concept for student housing combined with a public entertainment park turned out to be the most meaningful regarding long-term benefits. Since its opening this morning, the redesigned building already earned great approval by Berlin's inhabitants.

Bill of Data

Hilary Mason

Hilary Mason imagines a world in which anthropologists and ethnographers design AI and open source software, holograms and universally accessible computational systems are possible, and individual ownership of personal data is an accepted norm.

Back in the early 2020s, many AI systems were still black boxes—completely uninterpretable by humans. At the time, many people seemed to think that the best AI systems would be the ones that could make decisions on their own, while we deferred our responsibility to be a part of those systems to machines. And, of course, that didn't work out so well.

Humans built a bunch of these black box AI systems, but the systems were often biased. Because they discriminated, they could be used in ways that disadvantaged anyone who was an "edge case"—i.e., people who just didn't fit the perfect "average model" of a human being. But the truth is, that "average model" was an illusion. Nobody is average. *Everybody* is an outlier—in some dimension of their self, their existence, their identity. So, for a while, a future that relied on AI looked pretty bleak. But then, we created a new field, which evolved the way we approached building these systems, and paved the way towards creating the world we live in today.

This new approach was a blend of the best of the mathematics behind AI systems and the best inherent qualities of humanity. Instead of allowing the mathematicians and the engineers to drive what got built (and how, and when), we instead put the anthropologists and the ethnographers — the people who have the deepest understanding of human experience — in charge. Of course, this wasn't just a technical change; it required the creation of an entirely new discipline, and new processes for thinking about what was required to build AI systems that were actually interpretable, why this mattered, and what the implications of incorporating AI on a global scale were for our society.

It seems comical, of course, *now* — that we would have ever built systems that were not required to disclose how they work and what features they use, and that we, as individuals, had no recourse into understanding that data — but it took fairly significant regulation and legislation to change that. Legal requirements for AI systems now give individuals power over their own data, along with the ability to port that data from one system to another — but with the expectation that everything should be explainable in a way that allows us to take advantage of what AI and computers do best (which is to understand a scale of information that is outside the reach of our human cognitive brains and capacity), but then to reduce that scale of information, to help us make better and more informed decisions. This, in turn, allows us to live more human lives than we once did, when our society relied on systems that both discriminated against us and biased our decisions. The critical thought and ethical consideration that anthropologists and ethnographers brought to the table as they pioneered a new approach to building AI systems was foundational to our current way of life — which brings us to architecture.

It might seem, at first, that there is really no connection between the beginning of the field of architecture and the beginning of this new field in artificial intelligence. But today, we understand that there's actually a spectrum of environments in which humans operate. On the one hand, we have a physical world, which is completely disconnected from technology; in some places, we can still see and experience this. On the other hand, we have the world that most of us inhabit today, where the built environment around us is highly instrumented with sensors that constantly collect and process information, such that our environment adapts to our needs — and can even predict them! (Of course, we take a lot of this for granted.) There are also purely digital spaces that we now consider to be on the same spectrum of "places in which humans operate." The same kind of thinking needs to apply to how we manage our physical environments, the dynamic environments we've built, and our purely digital environments. It turns out that architecture and AI have more to do with each other than anyone once imagined.

For example, one of the most amazing moments for me was the first time I hologrammed into a space for a conference, which enabled me to fully participate without needing to travel. Before holograms were possible, we had video calls and other experiences that were really, really close — but they fell short of creating the feeling of being physically present with another person. Now, we have the wisdom and technology that allow us to project an illusion of our own physical presence into both digital and dynamically built spaces.

Getting to this point required a complete re-imagining of how architecture and digital technology could play together: connecting a vision for a world in which we can create a million realities for a few pennies with the understanding of physical space (and how humans interact with that space), and then building the software required to make it happen. It's been so cool to see that dream become a reality.

If you think back to the way we once thought about data as a good, and about the value that data had, we started with a bunch of theories, and it took us a long time to get to the right ones. We used to have this idea that data — well, it really did just belong to whichever company had collected it, and they could use it however they wanted. They could even sell your personal data without telling you! (We now understand this to be absolutely outrageous, but it was very common practice then. see also page 101 You'd catch a taxi cab on the way home late one night, and then, all of a sudden, your health insurance company would inform you that you'd gone to a bar one too many times, and they were changing the terms of your policy. It was ridiculous.)

So, for a while, we saw another movement against that sort of data abuse — a movement towards giving individuals ownership of their data, but one that tried to do so within a traditional, capitalistic model, where perhaps a company would pay you a few pennies to use your data. That didn't actually solve the problem.

But finally, we emerged into a more enlightened school of thought. A few brilliant thinkers, with a new theory of economics, came up with a system that integrates the value of data and personal privacy in less capitalistic ways. This led to the creation of an international and fundamental bill of data rights, by which we now always—obviously—have the right to see who has our data, and how it's being combined with other data. This bill of data also recognizes that data is a bizarre economic good, in that one piece of data alone is really not worth very much, but a "data commons" (where your data can be combined with other people's data, as well), holds great value. It really did take a whole new theory of the economics of data to understand how to harness that cohort, that social value—while still respecting the rights of individuals.

And so now, between our bill of data rights and our understanding of economic theory, we can feel fairly confident that our data is not being used in ways that we have not authorized. And, of course, we have the technological capability to understand where our data lives in those data commons, and to authorize and revoke authorization, when and where it suits us.

In the late 2020s, my company addressed the challenge of building computational systems that could interact with us as human beings in the same way—in the same interfaces—that humans use to interact with each other. At the time, we still had to sit at a keyboard, but we were typing commands that changed the way we spoke to qwerty computational systems. We built the core functionality that allows us to essentially have not *just* language, but also a *visual* interface with computational systems.

This had three significant impacts: the first was that it changed the experience of how we interact with computing and really open it up for a whole set of applications. Prior to that, unless you were specifically trained as a machine learning engineer, it was just awkward to interact with computers (and even then, it didn't always go well).

It also made a lot of data useful to us in a way that it hadn't been before. So now, for example, when you have a conversation with your doctor, you will always have the notes from that conversation to refer to at any moment in the future—without ever having to write anything down. Expanding our memories through digital tech is just one of the many ways that AI now supports us.

Finally, this new technology broadened its own accessibility. Previously, if someone wanted to build something, they would have had to program it themselves; now, anyone who can speak in any language (including sign language) can communicate with a computational system that will program it for them. Once the friction of that barrier was removed, we saw a flourishing of creativity in how people decided to use technology, and the future is now anything but bleak.

Hilary Mason, *orchestrated (eco)systems*

Hilary Mason, *Surfin'1*

Blaise Agüera y Arcas, *Surfin'2*

Francesca Bria, *Data vs. Space*

2037

Today, the best-seller-game *How Do We Want to Live Together?* has launched its second version which features data collection world-wide. The launching ceremony was held in an 80 feet diameter dome located on the roof of the Centre Pompidou in Paris, which is today partially used by the faculty of architecture of the Beaux Arts University. The dome was originally designed by American architect Buckminster Fuller for the 1967 World Fair in Montreal and has now been rebuilt by students and engineers. Fuller's idea of the World Game was a main reference for the programmers of *How Do We Want to Live Together?*

By the Sea

Tatiana Bilbao

It was more than fifteen years ago that the change happened. The skies had filled with grey clouds, heavy with ash. The raucous team of construction workers, always active and lively, had started to dwindle. Some had gotten sick, some had decided to move away from the rising seas on the coast. They were building an aquarium, a maze of concrete walls and long stairways and terrazas. There were giant tanks meant for colorful fish, and sharks and turtles from the nearby Sea of Cortez. It was filled with halls in which children would run from tank to tank in wonder, and where adults would recapture their awe of nature. Families and friends and visitors would fill the aquarium with their voices. But they never came, because on a cloudy day the construction workers didn't come back. The Structure stood, waiting — it was nearly finished, it was so close! That day the clouds burst and a torrent of rain started to fill the rooms of the Structure. This was just the beginning. As waves lapped at its edges, the Structure began a slow descent into the rising sea, and it knew then, it would never be finished.

It had been many lonely years dreaming of all the wonderful things that could have happened, only if it had been finished. Now, mostly underwater, the Structure's smooth concrete walls went from their soft brownish color to being smattered in some slimy green thing. If only someone would come back and take it off, it could be beautiful again. The slimy green on the walls turned into little blocks of anemones and smatterings of algaes. A slow invasion was occurring.

clitter clatter clitter clatter

Over the edge of a wall peeked a crab. It had a little pencil over it's ear and the tips of its claws clapped along the ridge of the wall.

"What's this here," it mumbled, before calling over its shoulder, "Come look, we can work with this!"

And over the wall came over a dozen crabs, exclaiming in glee. They had never seen anything like the maze laid before them.

"We can work with this, we can work with this," they chanted, as they picked at the walls inside of a room, creating divots of different sizes. 'Oh no,' thought the Structure, 'they will destroy my beautiful walls.'

The crabs settled down, having pockmarked all the walls in the room, and one by one they left. Feeling abandoned, and also sad that it was now damaged, the Structure let out a sigh.

Then it noticed, on the ground playing just above a mound of concrete pebbles, the most beautiful fish it had ever seen. With its little blue head, a shock of yellow and a brilliant purple tail, the little rainbow wrasse was enchanting.

swish swish swish

The water began to turn and move around and soon the room was filled with many rainbow wrasse. They swam into the caves in the walls and started to nestle in, creating little places to live.

146

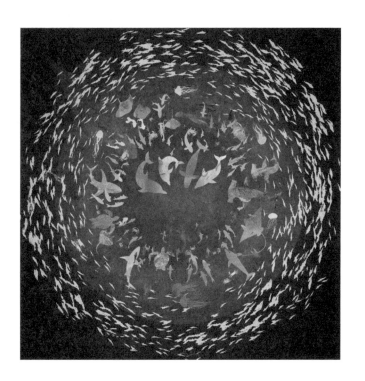

The crabs returned, with them a giant tortoise carrying corals on its back, glinting pinks and purples and oranges. The crabs worked with the school of rainbow wrasses' to fill all the holes in the wall with the bright corals, all the while saying, "Hello, neighbor, how do you do?"

The Structure had never seen so many creatures at once, and was intrigued to see how they worked together. In the flurry of activity, the Structure saw the old teaching the young, the young helping the old, creatures working together to make their houses. The old tortoise sat in the center of the room, contentedly munching on the green slime, happy to have helped in the way it could.

pop pop pop

Two big eyes peaked into the room, then one tentacle reached up, then two, then three, four five. A purple octopus pulled itself into the room, and surveyed the scene. The fishes and crabs continued building together when the octopus' eyes landed on the tortoise, munching away.

"Hmmm..." growled the octopus, "this would make a wonderful garden." The octopus loved to tend to sea gardens, filled with sea lettuce and algaes, all of the yummy things. With a garden this big, and the octopus' 8 tentacles, imagine what it could grow — it could harvest food for so many.

The octopus lumbered to the center of the room and called out, asking to share the room. "I will share with you my crops! And together we can dine on the finest sea lettuce," it's deep voice rumbled. The crabs and the fish readily agreed. They even offered to help with the harvest, because now with their houses made, they had spare time to join the octopus with its farming. It became an activity they could all share in, becoming closer and having elaborate dinners all through the week.

The Structure was captivated by all this movement, for it had been so lonely for so long. But the commotion in the room was attracting a lot of attention and little critters and creatures were becoming curious. Dolphins and fishes, crabs and turtles were also little by little setting up their own rooms throughout the aquarium.

There was so much space in the Structure to share, and other rooms were starting to fill with their own communities. Over time, little pockets of settlements had taken up residence in the abandoned rooms. In one was a music school, where dolphins squeaked and had theatrical performances. In another, a collective of crabs had created a whole library of tools for themselves; they loved to build and in their little room they had every sea tool you could imagine from sea hammers to sea saws. In another room some fishes had started an algae bloom playscape for their young and even another had some craftsfish making furniture for themselves. As each community grew they started bumping against each other and little kerfuffles were breaking out here and there between the rooms.

The Structure could see all the beautiful little homes and creative collectives, but these critters and creatures weren't sharing what they had made and what they really needed was a place to meet. The Structure knew the perfect place. It's door had been covered by fallen debris and with a sigh here and a rumble there, the structure began to tremble and the doors to the cavernous vaulted auditorium were uncovered. At the same moment, the dolphins could be heard squeaking, "We need to have a meeting! Through that door, we can gather and work together to build together!" They were always trying to tell the other fish what to do — they said it was because they were the smartest in the sea.

The dolphins led all the creatures into the auditorium, as the crabs, the builders they are, laid pebbles out in front of the door spelling out "The First Forum of Fish."

It was mayhem! The room was dark and everyone was bumping into each other. "Don't swish my tail," "Keep your claws off my shell!" "squeak squeak"

The school of lookdown fish realized that it was their time to shine. They looked to the dolphins who were trying to lead the meeting, and with a nod from them, all the lookdowns started to swim at the edges of the circular room, their silvery scales wobbling in the water, reflecting light.

Soon the auditorium filled with droplets of silvery light, and as the lookdowns swam faster, the whole dome shimmered alive. Calmed by the light, the First Forum of

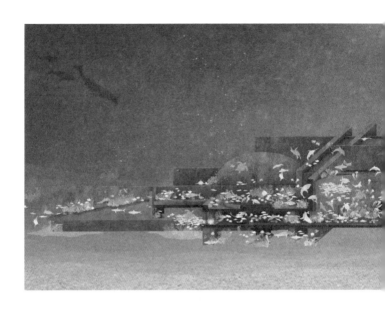

Fish finally began as the dolphins realized they needed everyone to equally share their grievances and hopes to truly create a working community. The first order of business was enacted almost immediately, and so the crabs studiously scuttled outside and amended their little rock formation to read "The First Forum of Fish and Other Creatures."

Though off to a rocky start, all in attendance soon realized that while maybe it was crowded before, and hallways were a mess, each of the little communities had something to offer and share. Seeing how the community of lookdowns shared their light, others started to participate.

Our friend the octopus let it be known that their collective had a lush harvest of sea lettuce with plenty to feed neighboring communities. A group of stingrays who had taken up residence at the edges offered to scout for new places to set up communities.

"We love to swim and scuttle on our own, we can help find new places to live! In exchange, you can share your treats," said a silky mantaray, showing off its wings.

As the chatter grew and agreements were made, they all realized they needed a place to exchange. The crabs understood that their tools were great for them, but could also be lent out to help build new houses and schools. The dolphins invited everyone to their school, while the fishes opened their playground to neighboring kids. Each community had something to offer. But where could they all meet?

The Structure was of course listening and knew the perfect place. It rumbled and trembled, it shook and sighed, and the young rainbow wrasse who had first played in its walls took notice. Really, it always knew there was something alive in the Structure, "It's telling us something," it exclaimed.

As the Structure huffed and hawed, it disrupted the sand and waves began to lead the fish through its maze of walls until they they tumbled into a gigantic open space with crystalline walls. It was the main tank of the aquarium, empty for so long, but now a perfect place for a market.

Zzz zzz zzz

An electric buzz descended from above, "We know how to make this a great market" burbled a jelly blob. A bloom of jellyfish gently swayed into the room, the creatures and critters surprised by their presence.

"We were listening to your plans," a jellyfish began, "you couldn't see us in the melee, "but we would love to join if you'll have us," bubbled another in the swarm.

zap zap zap

The jellyfish sent zaps through their tentacles, sparking electricity and decorating the market.

"We can work with this," chanted the crabs as they got to work building the market.

The Structure was filled with movement. Instead of the pitter patter of feet on the grand staircases, there were the enthusiastic swishes of sea creatures speeding through. Hallways were filled with anemones and corals and the friendly calls of neighbors. Activity filled the rooms with a farm here, and school of fish there. Little workshops making coral furniture were tucked into corners, and over yonder was a playground of giant pink sea sponges, speckled with seastars.

This isn't what it had expected, but at last, the Structure felt like it was a home to an ever-growing community.

Berlin, 2034, *complexity*

Berlin, 2034, *coexist*

Berlin, 2034, *Surfin'3*
Somewhere, 2034, *orchestrated (eco)systems*

Digital Peacekeeper

Audrey Tang

Audrey Tang looks back at the evolution of political systems and new technologies.

Back in 2020, people did not expect that it would actually be very easy to build common values even though we have different positions. So long as there's just the right mechanism to do so. We created a space where everybody can share their reflections about where the problem is, and instead of talking about how to fix it, we first had people share what they mean by fixing it, and what they feel about fixing it. This way, we reached a common map of the issues at hand. And very quickly people understood that there are certain pathways that are very thin, that are very difficult, but that there's a way out of the wicked problems.

Back in the twenties, people had the idea that we have direct democracy on the one side and representative democracy on the other, and that they're kind of fighting against instead of complimenting each other. In Taiwan, starting in the 2010s, we'd been prototyping a new political system in which, instead of two opposing systems competing on fixed resources like revenue, we had them work in conjunction with one another.

Participatory democracy was setting the agenda, like the first diamond in design thinking (which is, by the way, required reading for everybody educated in the 20s), and for the implementation — development and delivery — we applied representative democracy. Once we fixed the structure — the "how might we" question — and understood what democracy is supposed to produce, it became very easy for all the different

Audrey Tang, *History Channel*
Audrey Tang, *Surfin'2*

Audrey Tang, *Audrey Tang*
Audrey Tang & Omoju Miller

democratic systems to coexist. It could be a liberal democracy, it could be central democracy, it could be authoritarianism ... In short, we were capable of converging all of them into this new political system.

Previously, before digital, it was easy for a room with 20 people to end up agreeing on each other's values, but these 20 people were not capable to bring that feeling back to their comrades, back to their communities. Then the digital helped us make sure that people entered into an empathy space similar to that of face to face encounters.

Digital, by putting us in each other's shoes, allowed us to form this common understanding. And around the year 2025, quantum really helped a lot more. Now people entered this adjusted space, tailor-made to their personal feelings. They could voice all their fears, all their doubts, all their misunderstandings, all their uncertainties and participate in personal virtual conversation, with everybody not just trying to convince them, but also listening to them and providing productive feedback. With quantum computation, people suddenly felt that the Earth itself is talking to them.

Around 2020, we introduced this idea of the Internet of Beings. Not just people participating in democracy, but gradually, all around the world, rivers, mountains, animals and so on were included. All the different species capable of sentience, as well as ecosystems, were translated into avatars that speak on behalf of them. see also page 175 All these were included in the participatory deliberations that we talk about. Because of

164

technological restrictions, in the 20s these were mostly humans on the final decision implementation. However, including the environment and the social and future generations in the first diamond (ed.: *participatory*) was already helping a lot back then. By the thirties, we achieved pretty good sentience, quantum simulations of future generations as well as of the environment, so that now these actors can also participate in the second diamond (ed.: *representative*). Although this is still somewhat experimental at this point.

The market has been expanded, so that it is not just about trading services or products. We used the simple idea called quadratic voting, making sure that people understand that each of our strengths of preferences is best, if we just share our private assessments of common issues with the community, because this ends up resulting in the best possible outcome. As it was built on the idea that a person can only have a limited number of votes, one vote per candidate, this softened out the election paradox, the error paradox. (Previously the bits were insufficient, the uploaded information was not sufficient, and that is the cost of the paradox.)

When everybody switched to quadratic voting, people discovered that they can save their voting points, they can save their voice credits, and everybody understood, that it was the best for everybody to evaluate only the parts that they actually have an idea about, and also to learn from the analysis of other people that they care about, and that almost magically each increasing return of each vote is the same as the increasing expectation of the cost. And so, because cost and return are the same in this voting game, people aren't motivated to disclose their true feelings. And without a top-down distribution of political budget, a good, fair, sustainable distribution emerged in this market of votes.

In a zero-sum world, which was how it was in the bad old days, people followed the idea that resources are limited and they will have to compete in a win-lose mechanism. And because of the systemic imbalances, people who have lost made it a lose-lose mechanism to get revenge, basically. But using quadratic funding, quadratic voting and other methods designed by the radical exchange movement, we discovered that we can reverse the mechanism design if we are not playing game theory on zero-sum games.

Once you turn mechanism design into a participatory game, everybody starts devising games that are truly win-win for everybody involved. Because of that, people now engage in a lot more creative pursuits when it comes to politics. If people detect that there is a win-lose dynamic going on, they will say, "Hey, let's just have a hackathon and come up with a better mechanism" instead of focusing their energy on winning the game and making other people lose.

The Serenity Fork prompted people to have a new imagination about what a rough consensus based governance can do. Previously, people understood blockchain or Bitcoin in a very fixed term: The provider of a public ledger that is self-funding. That sounds okay, but it doesn't really expand to other parts of the society. But with Serenity, people now understand that the Ethereum naming system, for example, could be adapted and used for legal identities, too. Those legal identities don't have to come from a top-down government, bureaucracy or a bank, but rather it can be gamified. People or authorizers authenticate each other, using a distributed identity system or a social identity system. This is what we called it back then.

Nowadays, we just call it The Identity System. The old top-down, fixed, single point governance system was rendered obsolete, after the New Serenity system came about. It became one of the key points to enable people to have multiple jurisdictions and cross-jurisdictional identities. see also page 83 The idea of an alternate governance system became not something that you would have to rent an island for, but you can do it right away, in your existing communities, and it's compatible with existing contract law.

Imminent Communication with Nature

Mitchell Joachim

In the future, the natural realm interconnects complex emotions, values, and unambiguous messages to humankind. Elements within the world of nature cannot speak but they do transfer information. Humans have discovered symbols in the environment and are able to express the variable functions from nature. Every individual finds diverse implications in nature and recognizes wildlife differently. Nature is the voice of human awareness and how one comprehends the planet.

How can we actually correspond with nature? As we enter further into the future, biosemiotics becomes more prevalent. Biosemiotics is the combined study of semiotics and biology. It describes the prelinguistic meaning, creating, and interpretation of signs and codes in the biological world. Biosemiotics endeavors to incorporate the effects of biology and semiotics to offer an exemplary change in the scientific assessment of life, in which the knowledge of signs is one of its' embedded and deep-seated qualities. In the next few decades, humans will be able to speak with nature unimpeded through signs and codes.

Currently, it is common to perceive the natural sphere as somewhat separate from humankind. That we are individuals, and the environment is environment, and these are inherently opposite. Except we are equivalent. We all understand that the animal kingdom connects with us: we have either encountered this candidly in our personal lives, or seen it occur with others. Intermittently, this type of communication is astonishing: we have all heard the story of a group of dolphins saving a swimmer struggling in turbulent waters; the elephant that weeps upon being liberated from iron shackles; the devoted dog who greets a family member back home. Tomorrow, we will also communicate directly with the non-animal, non-reptilian biosphere, or rather the sentient plant world. And what about the non-sentient segments of the environment: the natural forces of air, water, fire, earth? Do they directly exchange thoughts and values with us as well? The resolution of course, is an absolute positive affirmation.

In fact, all entities, all materials communicate with humanity, though for purposes of this endeavor, will limit it to the natural realm, and all the mammals, beings, plants, habitats and climates that this includes. These are stunning, uplifting methods of communication with other animals: our species, part of our extended family. see also page 123

How is this achieved in the near future? There are many types of biological communication. Verbal and non-verbal: Verbal interaction is oral expression, either by interpersonal or mass communication. Nonverbal interaction is made up of speaking tone, body language, gestures, eye contact, facial appearance, apparel, noises, signs and symbols. These elements give innate significance and purpose to language.

By 2030 and beyond, signs in nature will persist with the exact same qualities found in anthropological literacy. Signs are especially critical in the environment. Signs are taken to function on a continuum, from 'iconic' with a singular firm connotation to users, through 'driven', to the truly 'subjective'. They vary along this fluctuating scale as to how cogently well-defined they are. In many cases natural signs have forceful enough inferences and suggestions to be at least partly 'driven'. When they are activated, they refer back to preceding predictable usages. Soon all of humanity will be able to read these natural signs and decipher their meanings. The world of tomorrow will have a deeper connection between society and nature. We won't need science to divine meaning from the ecosystem, instead anyone can just directly ask the flora and fauna within it.

Mitchell Joachim, 2019, *(eco)systemic1*

Daniel Schönle & Ferdinand Ludwig, *(eco)systemic3*
Daniel Schönle & Ferdinand Ludwig, *(eco)systemic2*

Daniel Schönle & Ferdinand Ludwig, *(eco)systemic3*
flamingoes, 2031, *The Negotiations*

It's 2038

terra0

In the mid 2010s a series of novel, locally-oriented governance structures emerged from the fringes of the net. Whilst early cases were mostly bound to virtual experiments with digital currencies and communities, the practice of building novel, self-governing institutions soon leaked out of the digital, spawning thousands of small holons governing physical infrastructure and land. terra0 was one of these early experiments; a prototypical example of the sort of experimental governance over physical, non-digital property that today is commonly handled by the sort of semi-autonomous infrastructure that began online.

The main insight gained from these early experiments was that, given enough time and resources, distributed technology allowed non-human actors to be properly integrated into contractual relations. see also page 161 Simultaneous to facing multiple mass extinctions, the societal awareness of ecosystems as a spiritual and material base for civilization grew. The subsequent retooling of legal structures led rivers to become persons and forests to become corporations. These early legal forms defining 'organisational-structures-as-persons' were quite crude; the disassembly of personhood as a hegemonic system of representation — which enabled the creation of more legally nuanced forms — happened later.

The rather simple question underlying this idea is, why stop at corporations as persons? Several nations have already enshrined or are in the process of enshrining rights for natural systems. Rivers, watersheds, coral reefs, mountain biomes, all could be represented by decentralized autonomous organisations, and the goods and services they provided defined in their charter. Might this be a better way to protect and promote the interests of natural systems and other species, rather than tying political actions to antagonistic ideological human-based movements?

Science fiction author Karl Schröder was unusually prescient in a 2015 post on the Ethereum Community Forum entitled 'Deodands: DACs for Natural Systems', published as these experiments began to emerge. Less than a decade later, the autonomous holons he outlined were brought into existence. The encoding of transparent rule systems into the management of ecosystems, coupled with the implementation of liquid and public voting systems, enabled the implementation of the first DACs.

After the publication of the terra0 concept paper in 2016, several small technical experiments were conducted. One of these was Premna Daemon—an autonomous Bonsai tree which paid the gallery space it was exhibited within for its upkeep. Another—Flowertokens—was a (controlled) attempt at generating the unique digital twins of 100 flowers, the data of which was kept in sync via computer vision analysis. In 2021—in cooperation with Sculpture Center in New York—a blockchain-based limited liability corporation was founded. The corporation leased a plot of land in New York, on which was a tree, and was represented by a smart contract. After the initial human owners of the corporation returned their shares to the corporation, it operated completely autonomously, with no human interaction necessary. Later that same year two other trees were added to the corporation, and by 2023 more than 5 plots of land across the globe were governed by smart contracts, mostly to provide natural conservation.

It took me some time to get used to the reversed relationship of dependency, but it stands to reason that it is more sustainable that way.

By this point, although the first institutions had also become interested, grassroots groups had begun to set them up on their own instance, each with their own set of rules. Localised networks in the Amazon basin — although different in size and scope than mutated forms of the network that had emerged in Northern Europe and Scandinavia — eventually began to interface with each other, via previously unknown instances that had laid dormant for years. The openness of the framework allowed for this — the western organisations belonging to the Non-Profit Industrial Complex no longer held the monopoly position and no longer governed the relation between people and their environment.

Vint Cerf, *Surfin'3*

Vint Cerf, *Surfin'1*

terra0, *terra0*   Vint Cerf, *Surfin'3*

Non-Markets and Solidarity

Evgeny Morozov at the World
Economic Forum 2038

We've developed a society not obsessed with competition. So, we forgot that competition used to be one of our main core values and goals, and instead we re-embraced the values that we have before us. Solidarity, cooperation, engaging in activities that are not driven by expectations of profitability, for example. That took a while, because the entire ideological and political infrastructure developed by neoliberalism, which has created all the mess we've been in, was there precisely to make competition the only value to be maximized within the political system.

It took a lot of time and we relied on three strategies. All of those strategies in one way or another were enabled by big data, digital infrastructure, artificial intelligence. see also page 131 So those three interventions took the form of designing non-markets, using solidarity as opposed to competition, as a discovery mechanism of new things, of innovative practices, techniques of production, and of using and leveraging big data and artificial intelligence in order to produce and allocate goods in ways that were actually superior to those of the price mechanism and the market.

Let's talk about each one of them in more detail. If you look, for example, at designing non-markets, it's obvious that new data intensive networks and digital infrastructures make it possible to coordinate human activity in new ways. It's possible for people to find each other. It's possible for people to find goods that others have. It's possible for people to find skills and knowledge that someone else possesses and organize a mutual exchange between parties without having to rely on the price, which has been the traditional mechanism of how goods were coordinated and allocated under capitalism. So, we have used the value of digital technology to actually bypass the key ingredient of the capitalist system and we have leveraged the communicative power of digital technologies in order to facilitate the kinds of exchanges that were traditional, and suppressed by the capitalist system.

We have also relied on a new source of innovative techniques. Traditionally, the neoliberal dogma that ran us into the ground, positive only in the way to uncover new things, to discover new inventions, to discover new scientific developments, was essentially to have entities compete with each other. Consumers had to compete with each other for better products. Companies had to compete with each other for profit and thus invest money into developing new tools of production and all the good things that we had. The capitalist theories that stalled us came from competition. This is of course never how society worked to begin with. In our everyday life, as we talk to each other, as we talk to our families, as we talk to our friends, we clearly invent new things.

We try to bring them into existence and you see that already, even in interventions like Wikipedia, a free and open source software, which are clearly extremely useful and innovative. They were not developed because somebody was driven by the logic of competition. Ultimately, we lacked the ability to scale up these kinds of interventions. We did not have the ability to have everybody engaged in this exchange and initially, we did not allow people to act on feelings of altruism or sociality that they might have experienced. With digital technology, it became possible to let them collaborate with each other. It served as an incentive to build all sorts of new schemes that formalized these collaborations. This of course allowed us to discover new ways of running our societies, of managing problems like climate change, and of essentially inventing our way out of disaster.

This has proven quite helpful and did not result in eliminating markets altogether. You need to decouple the idea of markets from the idea of competition. You can still have goods being sold. It's just that they do not need to be sold because if you don't sell enough you'll be out of business and you will have to close the shop. That last part is a direct result of the obsession with competition.

The last strategy that got us out of this mess was trying to design ways, which we have successfully done, of encouraging small producers, like artisans, or entrepreneurs. To take advantage of lost infrastructures like cloud computing, artificial intelligence, that have been turned from commodities, which they were under the last stages of the capitalist system, into the true public goods that they are now.

We've built a system, where essentially people who used to build apps, who used to build various small contributions to the digital economy, turned into artisans who no longer were at the mercy of Google, Apple or Amazon for the infrastructure. They used infrastructure as a public good. They could plan ahead, they could build very robust artisanal businesses around these things and they actually managed to produce things and get incentivized to produce them without having to worry about what would happen if a big digital feudal overlord would be angry with them. So, liberating them from the power of these big bosses was a right move, but also creating new ways in which they can discover each other, work with each other in tandem, and produce goods collectively was useful.

With these three broader design interventions, impulse interventions into the design of the digital economy if you will, a very different system came into existence. It all happened partially because of the ideas of a long forgotten cybernetician from Great Britain, Stafford Beer, who spent quite a lot of time in Chile working with Allende in the early 1970s, where he discovered and actually provided a nice theoretical background to designing systems that were robust, decentralized and tasked to deal with complexity.

Thanks to Stafford Beer, we have discovered the ability to manage complex systems by using technology itself rather than having to delegate that complexity out to the market or to the price system. see also page 91 And we discovered how to navigate this complex terrain by using technology itself rather than some second hand and inferior substitute like the market. Cybersyn, which is the name of the project that Beer ran in Chile, has been rediscovered and examined closely. It turned into a text book for those who were struggling to build systems for managing complexity for both national and global economies.

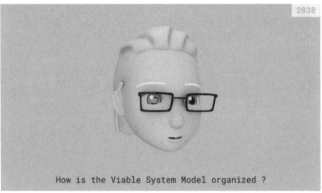

How is the Viable System Model organized ?

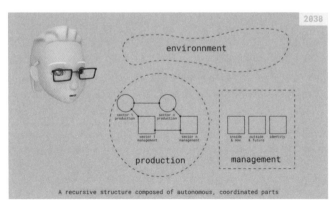

A recursive structure composed of autonomous, coordinated parts

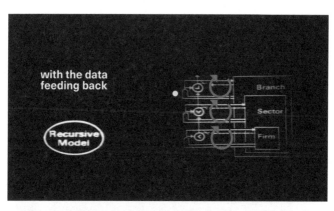

with the data feeding back

Recursive Model

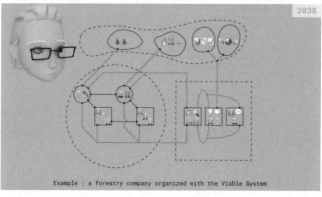

Example : a forestry company organized with the Viable System

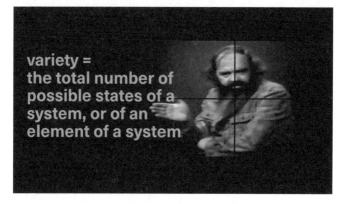

**variety =
the total number of
possible states of a
system, or of an
element of a system**

Inventing the End:
On Growth and the Artist

Joanna Pope

Feb., 2038

I

It is quite remarkable, our current culture of victoriousness. For all intents and purposes, we did win our war against the crisis. Our world is now replete with mostly carefully planned, mostly just, mostly degrowing economies, now winding down to their steadiest state. In our New Serenity, some even frame our victory as one over 'growth itself'. As one prominent geologist put it recently, these times "herald the end, if not of the Anthropocene, the Growthocene".

In such loose formulations like this, the Growthocene expands. It takes on the breadth of all of human history, and the deepest depths of human nature's 'dark side'—a tendency to compete, to conquer, to hoard and spread. Let us take a step back—the Anthropocene, after all, demanded that we think in longer time spans. Quite apart from the indigenous and autonomous communities that existed in opposition to, and were oppressed by, the growth paradigm and its agents until quite recently, many past human civilizations did not have a growth ideology.

Here I defer to the work of Gareth Dale, whose history of the growth paradigm revealed its absence in civilizations like Bronze Age Mesopotamia, India's Mauryan empire and Tang dynasty China. In Mesopotamian society, ostensibly "all ingredients were present necessary for the emergence of something that would at least bear a resemblance to the growth paradigm".[1] But in spite of the birth of agriculture, a Gilgameshian work ethic[2], the use of commodity money and sophisticated book-keeping, accounting[3] and even economic forecasting[4], a Mesopotamian growth ideology is nowhere to be found. The

Mauryan empire (322 BCE – 185 BCE) brought with it the Arthashastra, a treatise on statecraft and material gain that set out strategies for acquisitive projects to "ensure the royal treasury was full to the brim". [5] But its author Kautilya did not present wealth accumulation in terms of infinite, linear progress. Rather than "defending endless wealth or economic 'development,'" [6] the Arthashastra's logic was cyclical, embracing civilizational rise, fall and decline.

With its so-called 'Inexhaustible Storehouses' the Tang dynasty (618-907 CE) seemed, at first glance, to manifest "the quintessential capitalist imperative of continual growth", or something very much like it. [7] The Inexhaustible Storehouses were Buddhist monastery treasuries of monetary offerings from devotees, over time amassing large fortunes used for almsgiving, harvest loans and funding the monastery's own enterprises. [8] But what exactly was inexhaustible about the inexhaustible storehouses? Rather than "signifying the endless accumulation of interests," what was inexhaustible was the process of gift-giving itself. The 'quintessential capitalist imperative of continual growth' is one of increasing productivity, and corresponding increases in consumption. Tang dynasty's monasteries present us with an example of a gift economy, where one gift begets another. The aim was not to expand accumulation, but redistribution; to grow expenditure, not profits. [9]

The point of such historical excursions is not to unearth forgotten civilizational models that we might use as blueprints for our current post-growth era. Each of these past societies had their own forms of injustice. Mesopotamian states, often thought by scholars to have been "intrinsically better equipped to weather environmental or economic crises" by design, were also "built on high levels of institutionalized inequality" where resilience at the societal level was secured at the expense of the most vulnerable.[10] What Dale's work does remind us, however, is simply that ending the 'Growthocene' was not the installation of an unprecedented new world order. Rather, it was a desperately needed corrective on an historical aberration.

The history of the beginning of the Growthocene is none other than the history of seventeenth century northwestern Europe, when capitalist social relations and the colonial doctrine of progress became entrenched. Crucial episodes took place in the mid-1950s, when the (now thankfully defunct) OECD gave nations eminently exploitable narratives of economic expansion. As another historian of the growth paradigm writes, in the face of post-war problems of "rearmament, European reconstruction, political instability, colonial decline, and the Cold War... growth promised to turn difficult political conflicts over distribution into technical, non-political management questions of how to collectively increase GDP."[11] These histories are available to all those who seek them out, and if we are to believe our policymakers, will soon be taught in schools. But simply drumming these facts of the dawn of the Growthocene into our own heads won't suffice. What is also needed is greater attention paid to the history of the end, or many possible ends of the Growthocene, which is unfolding around us now. It is a truism to say that we cannot afford complacency, but I will say it anyway:

The growth paradigm is not behind us. This new world we believe ourselves to be living in exists only as an incredibly delicate balancing act, between decentralization and re-centralization and their multiscalar negotiations and rene-gotiations. This new world exists only so long as transna-tional solidarity exists, allowing processes of cooperation and autonomous self-determination to keep unfolding. see also page 181 Finally, until all reparations have been made to groups, human and nonhuman, past generations and future generations, who suffered and will still suf-fer the effects of under the destructive, self-destructive capitalism that relied on growth and its ideology for its survival, the Growthocene will still exist, and we will still be living, trapped, in its shell.

II

Stranger beliefs still about the end of the Growthocene persist in my own corner of the world. Not just that the epoch is dead, but about how we killed it. The politician or public intellectual will attribute our apparent revolution to practical policy interventions and new institutional designs that replicated and proliferated the world over. The radical will point to the political will of a united front of previously fragmented groups at the grassroots. A new generation of scholars now claims that it was all ultimately down to timing — just our luck in the cyclical patterns of rising and falling civilizations. All incomplete but reason-able explanations, each highlighting an important factor in a shift that none of us will ever fully understand. The same cannot be said for the explanation of the artist, who speaks only about the 'return of imagination'.

This much is odd — one might think that the artist is the ideal person to find ways to represent this chaotic combination of causal factors that brought about the New

Serenity. But the artist likes to look for a fundamental explanation, for the first cause alone. In doing so, she loses all nuance and finds only herself.

For the artist, our alternative world was only possible in the first place because people were finally able to imagine it. The artist celebrates the end of the Growthocene not for its own sake, but as the defeat of capitalist realism at the hands of a political imagination brought back from the dead. This imagination is a living, breathing utopian vision on par with that of the cosmists and Afrofuturists, and, in its flawless coherence, far mightier than the sickly, Frankensteinian appropriations and cooptations of the neoliberal and fascist varieties. The artist feels personally responsible for this victory. After all, it is the artist who is supposed to have the monopoly on imagination. Imagining is what she is best at. In the New Serenity, the artist is her own hero and saviour.

Perhaps, when writing a history of the Growthocene, one could include at least a detour that describes how this way of thinking among artists came to be. This little history would begin in the times before the New Serenity, when we saw its origins and inverse. Political artists saw the world through what you might call an imagination–deficit model. They were concerned about an apparent failure of imagination. They were not the only ones, in fact, failures of imagination were a common complaint, or to be more specific, a versatile rhetorical device. It was certainly a favourite of the military. The commission report into 9/11 chalked the attacks up to a failure of imagination. Once this imaginative deficit was rectified, a full US invasion of Afghanistan was no longer "inconceivable"; the global war on terror became possible.[12] A similar accusation of imaginative failure played an effective discursive role in the securitization of the global climate crisis, paving the way for an incredible expansion of the military–industrial complex to tackle the "climate threat" in increasingly destructive, bizarre and useless ways.[13]

But let us come back to the artist. What did imagination and its failure mean to them? For the pre-Serenity artist, living in times when it was supposedly "easier to imagine the end of the world than it is to imagine the end of capitalism," a symptom had become a root cause, and in turn, a wonderful beacon of false hope. The symptom: That it was "impossible to even imagine a coherent alternative" to capitalism.[14] It was a loose, rather general observation, true perhaps of Hollywood movies and a certain jaded contingent of the British and Continental Left. It certainly wasn't a fitting diagnosis for people fighting in different radical movements around the world, who were capable of both imagining a different world and attempting to realize it in miniature but replicable forms, creating autonomous zones that didn't seek to merely exit the system, but to continuously wage war against it.[15] Soon enough, these efforts too were rejected as manifestations of an inferior imagination and dismissed as "folk politics".[16] Moreover, the lack of imagination was itself portrayed as the sole reason why the pre-Serenity Left was failing in its efforts to meaningfully challenge capitalism.[17] The lack of a convincing utopian vision was the heart of the problem, and the most important dilemma to solve, and not the immense material advantage and unbelievably complex hydra of a system that held sway even as it seemed to be eating itself alive.[18] see also page 49

194

Precisely the same people who invented this diagnosis were the ones who claimed to have invented a solution to it — a political imagination, restored, by a vision of the future, invented anew. Of course, it was not a new future, but a rather tired one, worn out and full of holes. It was made mostly of productivism and reformism, along with gratuitous descriptions of technological silver bullets, from how synthetic meat is made,[19] or how carbon capture and storage works[20], all wrapped up in shiny exercises in speculation that seemed to serve the sole purpose of distracting from what should have been, by their own framework, a severe lack of political imagination.

Artists were captivated by these dubious visions, and soon fell into the same speculative trap of the pre-Serenity intellectual Left. But for them, such a trap had certain benefits that weren't to be found anywhere else. Nearly 25 years ago, the critic Boris Groys wrote the following:

"Art activists do want to be useful, to change the world, to make the world a better place — but at the same time, they do not want to cease being artists. And this is the point where the-oretical, political, and even purely practical problems arise."[21]

One such problem is that very little of what one does as an artist-activist, or a political artist, is of any significance at all. Of course, for some artists this is no cause for despair. Some are able to accept their own uselessness in this re-gard, and may even question why they should expect their art to have an impact comparable to that of a revolutionary movement or a supragovernmental body. Many artists are able to content themselves with engaging in non-artistic activism in which they do not play any special role, other than being an indispensable, anonymous member of a critical mass. But often, it is easier and more comfortable for the artist to dream of herself as deeply important, rather than embrace her own unimportance in the role of artist.

The philosopher Richard Rorty identified a similar phenomenon in the humanities of the pre-Serenity era, which he termed 'occupational alienation'. As one literary scholar put it, occupational alienation is

"that intriguing syndrome [that] occurs when one is so troubled by the awareness that what one does professionally may have very limited impact on the current political struggles that one begins to develop a self-defense mechanism which consists in believing something quite contrary, namely, that these professional activities have a profound value in this regard."[22]

This mechanism, arguably the driving force behind the speculative turn in pre-Serenity art, allowed the artist to protect her art from herself in the tumultuous years of uprisings and disaster until the New Serenity. And while the entire world struggled in the birth pangs of another era, this same mechanism saw the artist enter the new world with her sense of self-importance not shaken in the slightest. Everything is just as she had imagined it would be, and it was precisely her imagining that had helped make it so in one inexplicable way or another, a sibyl that had harnessed the full power of the self-fulfilling prophecy with next to no effort.

Do fantasies like this, I wonder, mean that the artist (or architect, or designer, or futurist, or any other creative practitioner) is still occupationally alienated, even in the

New Serenity? Why is it that they cannot bear to imagine that this new world was built around them through processes in which their role as artists had no tangible effect, other than perhaps as a hindrance, as their new visions and narratives provided an endless wealth of material for elites to pass off as their own in support of yet more exploitation, buying time for a desperate capitalism that sought to transfigure itself beyond recognition, a greener capitalism, a more inclusive capitalism, a capitalism for wellbeing, a capitalism beyond growth?

As an artist of some description, I can only ask my peers to be wary of the stories that we invent about our place in the world. They are no different from the comforting stories told so prematurely about the end of the Growthocene. Neither are bound to reality, nothing has ended yet.

1 Dale, Gareth. "Seventeenth-century origins of the growth paradigm." History of the Future of Economic Growth. Routledge, 2017. 27-51. P.28

2 Larue, Gerald A. "Ancient ethics." In: A companion to ethics (1991): 29-40. P.32

3 Ezzamel, Mahmoud, and Keith Hoskin. "Retheorizing accounting, writing and money with evidence from Mesopotamia and ancient Egypt." Critical Perspectives on Accounting 13.3 (2002): 333-367.

4 Woods, Christopher. "Contingency Tables and Economic Forecasting in the Earliest Texts from Mesopotamia." Texts and Contexts: The Circulation and Transmission of Cuneiform Texts in Social Space 9 (2015): 121.

5 Dale, 29.

6 Boesche, Roger. The first great political realist: Kautilya and his Arthashastra. Lexington Books, 2002. P.66

7 Graeber, David. Debt: The First 5000 Years. Melville House, 2011. P. 265

8 Dale, 30.

9 Dale, 31.

10 Paulette, Tate. "Domination and resilience in bronze age mesopotamia." Surviving Sudden Environmental Change (2012):- 163-191. P.183

11 Schmelzer, Matthias. "The growth paradigm: History, hegemony, and the contested making of economic growthmanship." Ecological Economics 118 (2015): 262-271. P. 266

12 "The 9/11 Commission Report: Final Report of the National Commission on Terrorist Attacks upon the United States." Air & Space Power Journal, vol. 18, no. 4, Winter 2004

13 Board, CNA Military Advisory. National security and the accelerating risks of climate change. CNA Corporation, 2014.

14 Fisher, Mark. Capitalist realism: Is there no alternative?. John Hunt Publishing, 2009. P.2

15 "Thus the 'TAZ', the alternative, the commune etc., are to be rethought, but with a critique of alternativism in mind: we must secede, yes, but this secession must also involve 'war'." Endnotes, "What are we to do?" In: Communization and its Discontents. Ed.: Benjamin Noys, Minor Compositions, 2011. P.30

16 Srnicek, Nick, and Alex Williams. Inventing the future: Postcapitalism and a world without work. Verso Books, 2015.

17 Fisher, 78; Srnicek and Williams, 3.

18 Biel, Robert. The entropy of capitalism. Brill, 2011.

19 Bastani, Aaron. Fully automated luxury communism. Verso Books, 2019. Pp.170-5

20 Buck, Holly Jean. After Geoengineering: Climate Tragedy, Repair, and Restoration. Verso, 2019.

21 Groys, Boris. "On art activism." e-flux journal 56 (2014): 1-14.

22 Malecki, Wojciech. "Save the planet on your own time? Ecocriticism and political practice." Journal of Ecocriticism 4.2 (2012): 48-55.

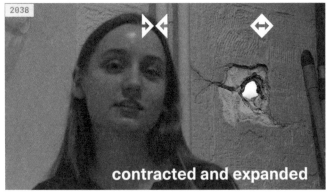

Joanna Pope, *degrowth world*

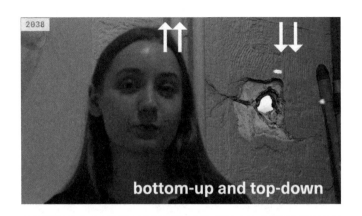

Joanna Pope, *degrowth world*
degrowth world

Hugs+

Leif Randt

May, 2038

MUNICH (2038) INDOORS / DAY

A low-pressure area moves across Germany.
May 27, 2038 is heavily casted by rain.
Kala Kade eagerly awaits her 18th birthday.
She grew up in the Bavarian eco-metropolis Munich, at the foot of the Alps, as the
daughter of a musician and a dramaturge
with German-Indian ancestry. If one would
ask Kala, how she felt about her youth so
far—which she has never been asked before—she would contemplate for a spell and
then reply: "I think most of the time I've
been fine."

She published her first own music in 2035,
being fifteen years old. In the meantime,
she has deleted these songs again. During
a four-week student exchange in the Metro-
politan Region Rhine-Main, a little more
than twelve months ago, she founded her
first band. With the keyboardist Aki Weyand,
the son of a Frankfurt artist couple, who,
just like Kala, will celebrate his eight-
eenth birthday in June 2038, Kala, who now
sees herself more as a songwriter than as a
producer, shares the dream to release their
debut record just before Christmas. Six
of the fourteen announced songs are already
finished, including two ballads.

Like every week at this time—it is 7
pm—Kala and her co-musician Aki have an

appointment for a hang-out. While the window of her small Bavarian teenage bedroom is sprinkled by rain, she puts on her simulation glasses and starts the Hugs+ software. On the basis of currently 800 selectable settings, Kala and Aki have chosen a simulation of the Berlin Gleisdreieckspark in spring 2021.

BERLIN (2021) OUTDOORS / DAY

Kala, who is wearing a light brown overall made of recycled fine cord, stands under a blue sky on the green park meadow and looks around searching. The park is not particularly well attended. It is the simulation of a rather quiet day in May 2021. People picnic in small groups or carry out strange individual sports. Some have put mats on the lawn and occupy themselves very seriously with stretching and breathing exercises.

  KALA: Aki!

Kala waves to a gaunt boy, who is wearing the old clothes of his father: light denim colours from head to toe. The medium wide pants are tied up with a belt below his bottom, the crotch dangles between the knee pits. The denim shirt ends exactly where the belt starts.It looks like Aki has enormously short legs.

AKI: Hey Kala. Have you been here for a while already?

KALA: No, I just tuned in.

Both stretch out their arms and put their hands into each other. They do not hug each other, but they hold their hands very firmly for a moment and smile at each other. Kala and Aki have met in Berlin in the early twenties a couple of times before. However, Kala and Aki never visit the turning point year 2023.

Musically, they are mainly interested in the twilight state before the transformation. Kala once formulated it as follows: The album should sound like a cry for help from a dystopian past. Although she has long suspected that many bands will sound like this very soon. But at least she wants to be the first to sound like this.

AKI: I've just been to the skaterglitch.

KALA: Again?

AKI: I just love it.

Aki refers to a skater, who, when trying to do a backside Five-O-Grind on the coping of the bowl an indefinite time ago, got caught up in a depiction error, and—unlike all other skate park events around him—stands still in frozen action. The highly concentrated facial expression of the skater gives the impression as if he's experiencing his frozen state with full consciousness.

AKI: Let's go to the cafe. Vincent said he had found a bug there, too. At one point, the waitress walks backwards.

KALA· May be that was in fashion back then?

AKI: Going backwards? I don't think so.

Kala and Aki stride across the meadow, towards one ultra-calm group of four people playing. It seems that the game is about hitting a little ball on a trampoline so that the opposing team cannot return it. Kala and Aki stand right next to them, but do not disturb their play because Hugs + simulations waive interactive moments. Nobody reacts to the presence of the two teenagers from the future.

KALA: My mother thinks that the early twenties have been a totally broken time. The rich were super rich and yet totally unhappy because there had been no more offers of meaning at all. And everyone else has slowly started to complain. About this and that. Discrimination, working

conditions, pollution, inequality. And
many were totally confused.

AKI: Were your parents sad, too?

KALA: No. They say they were doing rather well in that troubled time. And their
friends actually, too. In retrospect,
they find that almost absurd.

AKI: My birth must have completely over-
whelmed my father. I would have made him
blatantly melancholic, too. But when I
got three, in 2023, he would have realized
that not my birth was the subject, but
the reality of this hard time. And then
it went off.

KALA: Funny that you don't notice too
much of it here. May 2021. There should
still have been a pandemic.

AKI: Hugs + has not received the rights to
these horror images, I guess.

Aki is wrong on this point. It is rather
that the vast majority of users of such
a popular hang-out software like Hugs + has
no interest in getting together at places
that allow you to experience the horror
of the past. Because of this, Hugs + has
specialised on soft spaces like local rec-
reation areas and parks.

KALA: My dad once said that for a lot
of people that he knew the greatest
lifetime dream was to buy an own apart-
ment with two and a half rooms.

AKI: Why?

KALA: No idea. They thought it was cool
or something.

AKI: "A bizarre mix of paralysis and enthusiasm." That's what Vincent said about
our demo version of Hypnofantastic yesterday.

KALA: Paralysis and enthusiasm ..?
I don't know. Above all the song is
friendly, isn't it? Some just talk
too much. (laughs)

AKI: Totally.

KALA: I think that's why I make music.

AKI: I reckon you write good lyrics, too.

KALA: Thanks.

At the fence in front of the cafe hangs
an advertisement billboard of the running
shoe manufacturer ON. Run like on clouds,
it says.

KALA: Weird, that ON shoes already existed back then.

AKI: They even look better back then.
One of the pensioners that I look
after has exactly this model, I think.
Probably still original from the time.

Aki and Kala both participate in the
so-called points program in their districts—two afternoons a week Aki helps
out in a retirement home, Kala works
once a week with small children—that
grants them various free entries in the
entire district as well as discounted
pharmaceutical marijuana.

KALA: Looking at this makes me thirsty.

In the open-air cafe, young people of
the year 2021 drink Proviant cola from
glass bottles.

AKI: Do you want to take a short break?

KALA: Yes.

MUNICH (2038) INDOORS / DAY

Kala takes off her glasses and takes a
sip of water. It's still raining heavily
outside.

BERLIN (2021) OUTDOORS / DAY

Kala stands frozen next to Aki. At that
moment Aki sees the cafe employee walk up
three steps backwards. As Kala switches on again, the waitress walks down the
steps—pictured realistically.

 AKI: You just missed the glitch.

  KALA: That's ok. I think that's all
  intended anyway. You have to find
  something …

In the past few months Kala has grown
more suspicious of a critical search for
mistakes in popular simulations. Just
too many of her classmates have jumped
into this hobby recently.

 AKI: If you come to Frankfurt next week,
 I will have three new instrumentals
 ready!
  KALA: One is more than enough. You
  always plan too much for yourself.

 AKI: I'm just saying three so I can
 really get one done. (winks)

  KALA: Do you think you can tell that
  the people here were a lot more under
  pressure?

An immaculately trained jogger runs by in shoes from the brand ON. A father pushes a stroller towards the playground. Aki's glance follows both of them as he ponders.

KALA: I read that people in all forms of society have roughly levelled off in the same happiness degree which is inscribed into them genetically. So, most of the people in neoliberalism must have been as well as nowadays.

AKI: Statistically, a lot more people should have been mentally ill ten years ago. But my sociology teacher said that it is the definition of disease that has changed. Would you rather live in another time, Kala?

The blue hour occurs more abruptly in the simulation of the year 2021 than in the reality of the year 2038. Suddenly, it seems like a filter was placed on the scenery. Kala and Aki look around.

KALA: Is this normal?

AKI: I've never been here at this time my mother once mentioned that the sunsets appeared more dramatic back then.

KALA: I think you don't always have
to believe everything our parents
tell us.

The band duo sits down on a bench and looks
into the pink sky.

AKI: If we ever get famous, most
likely there will be a simulation, in
which you can watch us during our
first rehearsals.

KALA: And they will be presented completely wrong. (laughs) That annoys
me already.

AKI: My father wants to go out to eat with
me soonish…I think I have to go.

KALA: Sure, no problem. I'll see you next
week.

AKI: I pick you up at the train station!

Aki first freezes and then disappears.
For a little while, Kala sits on the bench
by herself. The sunset lasts forever.

the money was evolved
from trying to save banks
to trying to save the people

We built walls as well.

h trust. With networks of trust.

Elinor Ostrom

2038 — The visual is a trick!

2025 — we saved the internet

...et Governance Forum created a multi-stakeholder consortium of youth...

2038 — digital citizenship

215

Architecture is the Problem

Mark Wigley

May, 2038

Wachsmann was the key. Now, in 2038, it's obvious that there should not be architecture and should not have been architects. It's obvious, natural even, but it was really unnatural for a long time. There was a feeling that architecture is what made the human human. Architecture was this statement of how the human could organize and recognize itself. For a long time, we never listened to voices that said architecture is the problem. Konrad Wachsmann was one of those voices, constantly warning us about the dangers of architecture, and we didn't really listen. Then after the crisis of 2020, we started to listen for the first time.

Exactly 100 years ago, Wachsmann gets arrested in Rome because Hitler is visiting Mussolini on the way to opening the "Third Reich´s" German Pavilion in Venice. Actually, Wachsmann was arrested on both sides. First as a dissident German who has revoked his citizenship while in Rome and gets evicted from Italy. Escaping to France, he's promptly arrested for being a German. In the internment camp he starts to sketch a design for a lightweight hangar that he will develop as a refugee in the United States into what he calls a space frame—an ephemeral cloud-like mesh able to take any size or form to host any activity. So begins the idea of shelter that is not really a building, but what comes after buildings.

Wachsmann had already been traumatized by the horror of World War I. He was an apprentice cabinet maker, turned into a coffin maker by the mutual slaughter, before becoming an architect. He always had an acute sense of the all too human inhumanity of humanity and started to imagine the different society made possible by the transformative revolution of electricity, which becomes electronics. And electronics makes possible the thought of no architecture, no fixed lines, no hierarchy, no impositions. Nobody will know more than you know. Everyone will have all the information at the same time, seeing everything together and thinking collectively — continually collectively reshaping the lived world as ever pulsating flows of energy. So the idea of a static building in such a world disappears. Buildings become ghosts that linger for a while then fade away.

Wachsmann is one of the first theorists of dissolving architecture. Why he suddenly became so influential after 2020 is because there had always been this confusion about him. He seemed to only care about joints. Wachsmann had a cult following as the master joint maker and many architects thought "he's one of us," because architecture is how you put things together. They loved the drawings and the models: the ingenious joint of the vast air force hangar of 1950-54, for example, could bring together 21 different tubes at one point in any direction with just the blow of a hammer. But nobody understood that Wachsmann was so obsessed with joints because he thought the perfect joint would make architecture disappear. Instead of saving architecture, he's going to take it away. His argument was something like: "If I make the joints smaller and smaller, at a certain moment the building disappears. So, I can make a space frame as big as the planet, hosting all possible social transactions, but it's elements would be infinitely small, an invisible network of points in space, woven together with delicate threads. Solid buildings turn into flickering networks of points, and even a point is not a material thing but a potential. After all, there is always an emptiness, a hole, at the heart of every joint. The world after architecture will be made of networked holes." Wachsmann designed clouds that would fade. After 2020, everyone suddenly realized that the real lesson was not the hypnotically diaphanous cloud but the fading away.

Wachsmann's anti-architecture is nothing but an idea about democracy. Infinite connectivity is a spirit that's democratic in the sense that every point has the equal value of every other point. The connections and the network form the truth of the thing. Even what we used to call a building can be understood as a hole networked to countless other holes. And once you think of it as a connection point in multiple networks, it's not about the building anymore but the nets. In a certain sense, there is no longer any individual building or individuals within it. Nothing but net. It's radically democratic. But in a certain sense, there is no longer any individual, no discrete subject or place, just a vast interconnected organism. Wachsmann was asked in 1970, "What do you think about the invasion of privacy?" And he said, "I love it. Especially, television, which is a necessary invasion." He has the clear idea that the individual does not survive this process. First, that means the end of the individual architect. No individual makes decisions for others. The others make the decisions. And the others are a network -- a little bit human, a little bit technology. I think this gesture beyond the human, or the new form of the human that the human cannot yet recognize, is why Wachsmann is still a relevant figure in

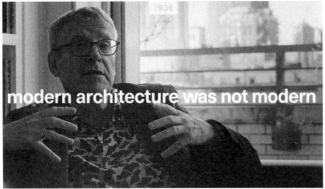

Mark Wigley, *A Crisis in Architecture?*

Mark Wigley, *orchestrated (eco)systems*

2038. His closest colleagues were figures like Buckminster Fuller and a few others. None of whom could easily be called architects. More like post-architects.

I think it's important to say that whenever I refer to Wachsmann: I am not really talking about a person in the sense of an individual, but the name of a TV program, a collaborative production — produced by a team, a team that even includes the audience. This golden lion is for a TV show. It's not just that Wachsmann thought that architecture was being replaced by television and actually devoted the last years of his life to being a TV maker. It's that Wachsmann, the very idea of Wachsmann, was always a TV program, a continuous broadcast. All the so-called radicals of the 60s were avid watchers of the Wachsmann channel: The Metabolists, Superstudio, Hans Hollein, Yona Friedman, Cedric Price, Archigram. But even they held on a bit to the old magical figure of the architect. It was only after 2020 that for the first time we took the Wachsmann broadcast seriously, a broadcast about life in the age of broadcasting.

Was this an invented effect of architectural historians? I'm a bit suspicious of these histories, the Wigley book on Konrad Wachsmann's Television from 2020, for example. But maybe the question whether Wachsmann was a person or a collaborative effect was always there. Was Wachsmann an architect, or a post-architect? Think of the summer house for Einstein, the project that put the name "Konrad Wachsmann" on the map in 1929. It always had a mythological quality, and was even about the production of a myth. A beautiful wooden house, in the trees near the lake on which Einstein used to sail, was an image of being disconnected from technology but this building was manufactured in a distant factory where Wachsmann was chief architect. The wood was cut into modular units by machines in the factory, the building was assembled inside it, taken apart, put on a truck, taken to the lake as a kit-set and reassembled. So nothing could be more technological than this structure produced as an image of detachment from technology. We have the very beautiful photograph of the Einsteins sitting with Wachsmann on the porch. As Wachsmann recalled in his very last text, Einstein thought that electricity would not change architecture. But the young architect was already sure that the new flows of energy and information would revolutionize architecture. I think he never knew what would replace architecture. He just knew it would leave and his responsibility was not to design architecture but to design its exit. The one remarkable vertiginous drawing of a twisted net Wachsmann made in 1950, the drawing that haunted him for 30 years, was an attempt to visualize the kind of the portal through which architecture would leave.

It was very interesting how the architect as a species survived into the 21st century, perhaps precisely because it is such a retroactive discipline. What they used to call modern architecture in the 1920s was not an embrace of the technological revolution of the 19th century but an anesthetic to deal with it. So modern architecture was not modern. It was a way of not being too shocked by the fact that everything had already changed. So maybe it made perfect sense that we still had the figure of the architect deep into the 21st century before the crisis of 2020. We still had this figure of the architect because there was still this need to absorb the shock of electronics. Architecture was still presenting life as seen through the rear view mirror. The loss of architecture after 2020 was the loss of thinking that you know or could know or even want to know what comes next. You no longer have buildings to protect you from the shock of the present, which is its uncertainty precisely.

Already in 1948, Wachsmann stood up in a conference of most of the modern architecture mafia saying basically: "Energy is everything. Energy is now electricity. Electricity changes everything. And electricity will be wireless. It will be broadcast. Building gives way to broadcast." This is the same argument that Buckminster Fuller had made since the late twenties, including the idea that energy will come through the air. What you used to call a building is just a way of redistributing this energy. The energy is also information. So we live inside electricity taking the form of electronics, living a life that cannot be predicted, a life that will be always constantly reacting to our desires. Not just a world without buildings but a world without architects, since the future is precisely that which cannot be visualized. The future is by definition unexpected. The future, by definition, comes after architecture.

The classical figure of the architect was that of a documentarian. Statistically, architects were only ever engaged in about 1% of the built fabric of the world. So they were never really making buildings or cities. What they did was to produce images of stability as a kind of counter to all the instabilities. Architects survived way beyond their expiration date because the electronic systems they were belatedly engaging had been revolutionizing human and non-human life since the mid 20th century. So somehow the idea of the architect as decision maker — drawing lines that supposedly shape contemporary and future life but actually tracing the outline of long established life—lingered on. The figure of the architect paradoxically survived even when visualizing the systems that undo that figure. But 2020 made the desire for a stabilizing image-maker seem almost immoral.

Yet as a historian I noticed that a desire for the lost figure of the architect started to grow in the early 2030s. Why would we need somebody to visualize the present when everything comes to us in real time in such complex ways? When the we is not just we as humans, but we as bacteria, plants and technologies, programs and protocols? When the we is so massively complex? Why would we want to slow down and see a visualization of the situation we're already in? Yet I notice this itch. I feel it.

After all, we still come to Venice, to have a conversation every two years about "What was architecture? What has it become?" At first it was a kind of a funeral: Architecture is gone. Now it has become a collective call for the possible reconstruction of the idea of the architect. Increasingly I am being asked to talk again about the manifesto of Wachsmann. In the moment that we want to recover the figure of the architect, we want to look at the history of the loss of that figure. I'm reminded of Erewhon, the book of Samuel Butler from the late 19th century. Erewhon is a play on the word nowhere spelled backwards. Butler writes about somebody in New Zealand who wanders across a mountain and comes to the other side and is arrested for wearing a watch. Why? Because it's technology. The society on the far side organizes itself around The Book of Machines by a philosopher that describes how we made watches to help us tell the time just as we make all our technologies to be extensions of our brain and bodies. But after a while we become the servants of these prosthetic extensions that start to breed amongst themselves and the human species may become extinct as the machines take over. Erewhon is a manifesto about machine life that has an ambiguous ending. I wonder if the Wachsmann manifesto is something similar. He writes about the disappearance of architecture and the figure of the architect as part of emergence of a new hybrid species. And maybe we are looking at these texts again now that we have not had architects for a generation and are gathered again in Venice like members of a cult wondering whether to reconstruct the old species in our labs.

Deane Simpson, 2038, *coding, changing, learning*

Deane Simpson, 2038, *A Crisis in Architecture?*

Deane Simpson, 2038, *coding, changing, learning*

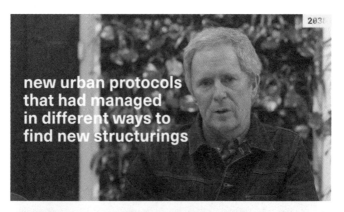

new urban protocols
that had managed
in different ways to
find new structurings

an entirely new set of layers

trust-based society

Deane Simpson, 2019, *Data vs. Space*

Deane
20 years before

Remember Big Tech?

the BIG 5 were

Amazon
Apple
Google
Facebook
Microsoft

The State and Status of Fishes and Aquatic Invertebrates: A Retrospective

Jennifer Jacquet and Becca Franks

Department of Environmental and Animal Studies, New York University

Annual Reviews Further

Click here to view this article's online features:

- Download figures as PPT slides
- Navigate linked references
- Download citations
- Explore related articles
- Search keywords

Sep., 2038

Keywords
cellular seafood, fishes, fisheries, reciprocity, sanctuary, social
change

Abstract
We reflect on the profound transformation over the last two
decades in society's relationship with fishes and aquatic invertebrates, animals who were often previously referred to as simply
'seafood' and killed at now unimaginable rates: at its peak, trillions of individuals per year. A combination of rapid changes in
scholarly research, pedagogy, technological developments, and
youth-driven, animal-related campaigns and activism, provoked
political will at national and international levels. We highlight
some key moments in the transition to embracing a reciprocal
relationship with fishes and aquatic invertebrates, including the
changes in marine biology and ecology curricula to incorporate
perspectives on individual animals (not only the species-level
view that previously characterized the fields), the decision by
major media outlets to adopt a new language (e.g., referring to
'fishes' instead of 'seafood'), and the role of architectural design
in enhancing our interspecies interactions--to the benefit of
aquatic non-humans and humans alike. In terms of political
action, the key developments were the elimination of fisheries
subsidies at the WTO and the protection of 80% of the oceans,
including designated no-entry zones. The leadership of Queen
Victoria of Sweden, civil society groups, especially youth activism in Korea, China, and Japan, and technological developments, including the creation of affordable, nutritious and
wildly-popular 'animal-free' seafood products, all made major
contributions to ending industrial fisheries and the expansion
of animal aquaculture.

Introduction

Our modern, mutually-beneficial relationship with fishes and aquatic invertebrates is now so predominant and pervasive, it is easy to forget that until recently, we exploited these animals at an unprecedented global scale. For example, in 2018 alone, hundreds of billions of individual carp, salmonids, crabs, shrimp and other aquatic animals belonging to more than 400 species across six phyla were farmed for human consumption[1]. In the same year, another 110 million tonnes of nearly countless aquatic individuals were captured at sea and subsequently slaughtered or simply discarded as 'waste'[2]. The industrial fishing fleet, which included nearly 40,000 factory trawlers, accounted for at least 75% of the global fish catch and resulted in the destruction of seafloor habitat and bycatch of countless turtles, sharks, and seabirds [3]. All this destruction to aquatic life reaped few necessary gains: only ~3% of the global tonnage was caught by subsistence fisheries to feed food-insecure people; the rest went to luxury or food-secure markets or secondary applications, like animal farming [2]. The trillions of animals killed in this process were thought of merely as 'seafood' and fisheries science focused on maximizing profits or, at best, making fisheries 'sustainable' for continued exploitation. Shifting the moral calculus on a global scale required no less than a revolution in science, education, technology, social norms, and built structures, but was achieved with unexpected speed through the effort of multiple actors and the collective realization of the benefits of a relationship in which both humans and aquatic species could thrive.

The picture from twenty years ago is almost impossible to imagine today. Our relationship with aquatic animals, especially fish and invertebrates, has been completely transformed. Here we trace this recent history and highlight some key events that contributed to this shift. We begin by recounting the relation-

Jennifer Jacquet & Becca Franks, *(eco)systemic2*

The Timbuktu Files

Lukas Kubina

Nov., 2038

On the shores of Lake Turkana, my grandfather and I sit by the barbecue and bathe in the twilight of a violet sunset. While piling firewood, he starts reminiscing over dark times. He pulls me into a past in which African countries were considered periphery, patients of the world economy at best, disconnected from the 'first-world' and perceived as causes for migration problems. "They were viewed as a pain to be protected against. With walls, fences, and Frontex. It's a true story!", he insists. "Today, language doesn't have these concepts anymore. see also page 15 You would have to visit one of the reserves, where there are still people who haven't left the market-centric psychology or its syntax and vocabulary."

In fact, I did. Once, I visited the eco-metropolis Munich, my grandfather's birthplace, physically. When I heard about the reserves in the Alps, I couldn't resist and took a train to Salzburg. At the gate, signs were suggesting how to interact with the inhabitants: "Don't expect public goods! Don't question their beliefs! Act friendly! Don't take LSD — it is prohibited by the local authorities!"

Today is the 10th anniversary of the Timbuktu Files. Grandpa loves telling me about their importance. He's done so countless times before, but their mystery never gets old. And I just love hanging out with him. His happiness feels so different compared to my generation's, somehow more relieved rather than relaxed.

I know more or less what's coming: The Timbuktu Files are a large collection of manuscripts about art, medicine, philosophy, and science that were preserved in private households since the 13th century. Throughout time, they were saved by brave bureaucrats, hidden from the torches of bigotry, and juxtaposed against a colonial mind-set. On the one hand, I think Grandpa simply enjoys story-telling. On the other, I assume he wants me to understand that I should never take anything for granted — although everything now is, kind of.

"The Timbuktu Files were collated and made open-source when Europe disintegrated and retreated into a fragmented standstill. Just after the jackpot in 2023. You have to keep in mind that the European Union once had been the flagship of hyperlocal supra-nationalism. A bit premature, a bit opaque and sabotaged by particular interest. But hey, at least they tried. Then, borders reappeared and were closed, public life caved in, and the political sphere was under anesthetic. The whole continent retreated to the privacy of four-walled homes. At that time, while Europeans were beating on pots and pans, the African Union not only picked up the principle of supra-nationalism. They were also rediscovering ancient paths to lead the way."

While listening to my grandfather's soft voice, I recall that a series of rare events led to the complete breakdown of societies and economies across the globe almost 20 years ago. They exposed the vulnerabilities of the old regime but before its extremest absurdities were overcome, the world was paralysed for a while. Basically, people retreated to privacy and looked into the abyss. As far as I remember, this era is commonly known as "The Renaissance of Biedermeier".

"More than half a decade after the first implementation of the viable system model in Allende's Chile, the combination of Stafford Beer's ideas see also page 91 and block chain technology was born here, on the shores of this lake. The machine learning community, which was originally leading the systematic understanding of the Timbuktu Files, sat down in the value village Nariokotome and designed the prototypes." Grandpa points vaguely towards the North. A few Nile crocodiles paddle across the horizon. "These prototypes have evolved to be the best-practice, self-repairing, steadily-evolving blueprints for autonomous systems. Afrofuturism has always shown solidarity and transnational thinking. At times, when Europe and the so-called 'first-world' lost unity, the African Union got stuff right. Now, their models are distributed and implemented on a planetary scale."

I am still a bit puzzled by his ironic terminology. What does 'first-world' exactly mean? Even though I've heard it many times before, I still cannot wrap my head fully around it. He takes notice of my confusion with sympathy and gently rubs my Max Weber tattoo. It feels like he's utterly pleased.

"The digitized Timbuktu writings led to a rediscovery of the Pan-African cultural and scientific heritage. And it's been only a few years since they were understood by the rest of the world. Acceptance and tolerance had not been a strong suit before." His face morphs into one extra-large smile. "The tipping point was when the machine learning community across Africa shared the decoded knowledge in the papers with the world freely."

He then turns on the daily telecast of the President of the African Union. Omoju Miller is addressing the anniversary, too:

"The knowledge from our datasets has helped us to completely reverse the impact of climate change. Also, we no longer have the migrant crisis. People are thriving in their own homes. This technology has revolutionized life on Earth to the point that no one is thinking of making humans multi-planetary as a form of supporting life outside of Earth."

The telecast fades into twin holograms as Juliana Rotich, Minister of Economic & Social Affairs of the African Union tunes in.

"Think about the laser beam of human effort, that laser beam being composed of technology enabled governance, technology enabled participation, technology enabled collaboration and using technology to actually solve problems and pointing all of that onto actual real-life problems."

The lake gleams Patagonian. The moon is blue. Tonight Jupiter and Uranus meet each other three times. The telecast flicks back to Omoju Miller, who now sits in the shade of a massive Baobab tree, in a forest of all sorts of trees, Buffalothorns, Bushwillows, Jackalberrys, Knob Thorns, Marulas, Mopanes, Tambotis, Jacarandas, Welwitschas and German Oaks. In the background, Ouroboros meanders between the tree trunks, and, with a full mouth, her soft mumbling ripples in cosmic circles. The President of the A.U. says:

"The best thing that happened was planting all those trees in Northern Nigeria and seeing the complete reversal of desertification and the impact of that reversal, reversing the entire effect of global climate change. Realities have changed. All the species are back, because their habitat has been restored. Extracting the DNA sequences from plants assisted in the development of all kinds of cures to previously chronic and terminal diseases. The current life expectancy — with full mobility — of humans is now 111 years — female and male alike. The transformative power of ancient wisdoms across the African continent changed the way how we live on this planet. Imagine, in the late 2010s one of the biggest challenges we had was global payments. I remember not being able to use my mobile app to pay for goods in Dakar as I used to do in Lagos. Nuts, right? Once we cracked the thing, we built a system that allowed us to do payments anywhere across Africa. As it turned out, that system and The Timbuktu Files unified all of us. It ended up creating an experience of a Pan-African reality such that even our former governments had to get on board. And finally, we created an African Union that was truly continental. The things that the Europeans were trying to do with the EU, we achieved them in Africa. Through software. We realized that humans can work cooperatively. On a software platform that became the viable system. Sharing it globally, it became how the world actually convenes. The first milestone for the planetary system was the collaboration with the New State in 2031 ... " see also page 49

Grandpa switches off the telecast and we share a pleasant moment with our own thoughts. A lion roar cuts through the air. The coEXISTence app hasn't sent a message yet but I check anyhow. Easy, we are not in the predator's territory for the next hours. Suddenly, I feel the urge to tell him about my trip to the reserves. Something which I haven't done before.

"It was bizarre. The inhabitants owned very big vehicles. And it seemed like that odd fact made them proud and happy. They drove them from their private homes to lifts that were just a walking distance away. On top and at the bottom of the mountains, they were gathering in small tents and listened to noise that they could only cope with because they intoxicated themselves with alcohol. On the slopes in between, it was social Darwinism. At nighttime, you could not see the stars because of all sorts of fireworks and the valley was filled with the sound of machines that were producing artificial snow for their sport activities. It was very stressful."

My grandfather listens carefully. After a little while, he looks ... me in the eyes and lays his hands on my shoulders. "It was close. We almost didn't make it. But we did. No more drama, Max. Let's go for a swim."

2038

the knowledge we found in the Timbuktu Chronicles

2038

extracting the DNA sequences from those plants

Omoju Miller, *The Timbuktu Archives*

The Plant, *The Timbuktu Archives*

Omoju Miller, *The Timbuktu Archives*

Juliana Rotich, *The History Channel*
Omoju Miller, *The Timbuktu Archives*

The Future is Present

Ludwig Engel & Olaf Grawert

The future is not a time. It's a tool to deal with time and as such it is the most openly discursive and democratic narrator we can deploy to actively engage with the present. The future is anchored in our present as a narratological tool, which connects individual and collective experiences of the past with each own's and societies' expectations of the coming times. Thus, a story about the future is always also a story for the future. Because it adds another narrative aspect to the repertoire of what is currently conceivable about the future and changes the possibilities of what the future can be.

2038's effort can be read as a story from the present for the future and thus, as a present to the present. Despite the prevailing vision of a negative time ahead of us regarding basically everything from society to nature, from the intraplanetary to the interstellar, 2038 set out to tell a decisively inconsistent story. Of a somewhat better future, that is. 18 years from now. In 2038, not everything is golden and easy but neither foul and irrevocably bad.

The approach follows a principle of hope, setting a positive scenario to reverse-engineer the present, reframing the contemporary as a laboratory. A laboratory that already possesses the tools and ideas necessary to overcome the dystopia ahead. Far from naivety and utopian positivism, 2038's research does not look for a formula to press all findings into a coherent system but rather takes on the task to deal with all the strange little artifacts, which possibly could trigger systemic change and tell the story as contingent, complex and paradox — as it is. The past was messy. The present is messy. The future will be messy, too.

Part of 2038's concept was to ask experts to tell their story as they were living in this very near future. A time in which the system has changed for the better. The only rule was to be serious about it: committed and transparent in argumentation and humble in their approach, as to say: *I'll let you be in my future if I can be in yours.* This is really important. When one talks about the future, never shirk the responsibility. *Skin in the game.* What one describes and articulates in all seriousness, should not be an escape from the present but rather the sharpening of the point that one wants to discuss, the question one wants to raise, or even the answer one wants to speculatively anticipate in the present. Claims about the future, strategic maneuvers for a certain future over all others must be avoided at all costs. Because a utopia or a positively conceived future-idea is always only a stimulus for self-reflection and action. If it is meant to suppress other futures — positive or not — it becomes totalitarian. In that sense, 2038 is rather a set of action-guiding ideas that must never be literally translated one-to-one into the present. It is important to distinguish between idea and execution. *Beware of you dreams, for they may come true.*

The present always includes past futures. Everything that has been imagined to one day become the present but has not materialized yet, exists in a non-time limbo as a utopian ghost ready to haunt you. To start with a thorough investigation of the present, thus means to identify the utopian ghosts that clog up our speculative capacities to transcend the present. Speculative fiction is a space of relief. A story, set in the future offers to become such a space. But given the current situation — we are writing this in the summer of 2020 — it has become difficult to continue to function as before, in this very different present. Time has accelerated, again. The story 2038 created, has become outdated before it could be confronted with the time that informed it. It turned out that 2038 not only was set against the backdrop of three recent global crises (financial markets, migration, climate) but on the verge of the next crisis looming. 2020's crisis is also a crisis in visionary thought. Planning for different futures has become obsolete because we already live in scenarios. Even the planning of the present has become impossible. This uncertainty toward the even near future renders the most recent speculations irrelevant and rejuvenates past futures.

Wouldn't it be nice to find the answers for today in looking back at visions of the past? Beware, to look back in time and revive what has not happened, might seem the easy way out. It is no way out, after all. The most future-oriented thing you can do right now is to celebrate the moment, be in the now. *We love our time.*

Being part of 2038 we continue to be slightly optimistic. Sure, the general conditions have changed drastically; the public discourse and public attention have shifted, yet, the problems are still the same. Answers to "How can we live together?" have just become even more rare and needed then they already have been before. 2038's platform now functions as a seismograph documenting the eruptions of the very near past. A fragment of yesterday's present that—if not documented properly—would have been eradicated by the massive global shock. Yet, 2038 is so much rooted in the now that it has not yet lost its glow. But the reading is certainly different: It is a historical document now, a history channel of a present that never was. 2038 is now here to inform this new present about alternatives, hopes and diversions to challenge our thinking and estimation of the contemporary, and to develop a fresh baseline from which to think anew.

dymaxion, *The History Channel*

Llama, *A Crisis in Architecture?*

Yona Friedman, *complexity*

E.Glen Weyl, *The Property Drama, again*

how we see the world around us

2038

future

chicken, *coding, learning, changing*

Agave, *coexist*

Video Index

Video Team

Memojis & Aging
Jan-Peter Gieseking, Jan Bauer,
Tobia de Eccher

Colours
Severin Bärenbold

VSM & World Game Drawings
Benjamin Burq

Recordings
Sonja Junkers, Lukas Kubina,
Olaf Grawert, Christopher Roth

Worlds
Julian Wäckerlin, Pan Hu,
Christopher Roth

Team 2038

2038 is an international team of architects and artists, ecologists and economists, philosophers and politicians, scientists and writers, initiated in 2019, aiming to tell a (hi)story that today we call future:

Blaise Agüera y Arcas, Diana Alvarez-Marin, Andrés Arauz, Arts of the Working Class, Mara Balestrini, Sandra Bartoli, Diann Bauer, Jan Bauer, BBSR, Carl Berthold, Tatiana Bilbao, Lara Verena Bellenghi, BMI, Oana Bogdan, Erik Bordeleau, Mohamed Bourouissa, Arno Brandlhuber, Jakob Brandtberg Knudsen & Lorenz von Seidlein, Francesca Bria, Loren Britton, Agnieszka Brzezanska, Vera Bühlmann, BUREAU N, Benjamin Burq, Marina Castillo Deball, Vint Cerf, Steffi Czerny, cfk architetti, Kristof Croes, Elke Doppelbauer, Keller Easterling, Tobia de Eccher, Ludwig Engel, Joao Enxuto & Erica Love, ExRotaprint, Manuel Falkenhahn, Jan Fermon, Cosimo Flohr, Foreign Legion, Yona Friedman, Renée Gailhoustet, Jan-Peter Gieseking, Goethe-Institut, Olaf Grawert, Dorothee Hahn, Sophie von Hartmann, Helene Hegemann, Holger Heissmeyer, Angelika Hinterbrandner, Nikolaus Hirsch, Fabrizio Hochschild Drummond, Ludger Hovestadt, Pan Hu, JUNG, Jennifer Jacquet & Becca Franks, Mitchell Joachim, Sonja Junkers, Roberta Jurčić, Claudia Kessler, Goda Klumbyte, Gábor Kocsis, Sénamé Koffi Agbodjinou, Ulrich Kriese, Lukas Kubina, Nikolaus Kuhnert, Phyllis Lambert, Samira Lenzin, Lawrence Lessig, Cédric Libert, Ferdinand Ludwig & Daniel Schönle, Suhail Malik, Charlotte Malterre-Barthes, Renzo Martens, Hilary Mason, V. Mitch McEwen, James Meadway, MicroEnergy International, Omoju Miller, Evgeny Morozov, MOTIF, Motor Productions, Caroline Nevejan, Bahar Noorizadeh, Sabine Oberhuber & Thomas Rau, Jorge Orozco, Verena Otto, Shwetal Patel, Wong Ping, POLIGONAL, Joanna Pope, Christian Posthofen, Leif Randt, RAUE Rechtsanwälte und Rechtsanwältinnen, Rebiennale, Kim Stanley Robinson, Denis Roio, Raquel Rolnik, Meghan Rolvien, Christopher Roth, Juliana Rotich, S.a.L.E. Docks, Saygel Schreiber & Gioberti, Patrik Schumacher, Jack Self, Max Senges, Deane Simpson, space-time.tv, Jonas Staal, Bruce Sterling, Michael Stöppler, Lia Strenge, Audrey Tang, Terra0, The Laboratory of Manuel Bürger, Cassie Thornton, Jeanne Tremsal, Galaad Van Daele, Iris van der Tuin, Marcus Vesterager, VITRA, Julian Wäckerlin, Moritz Wiegand, Eyal Weizman, Julia Werlen, E. Glen Weyl, WHY Ventures, Mark Wigley, Anna Yeboah, Erez Yoeli and Tirdad Zolghadr.

This publication is based on the idea of, and was developed in parallel to

2038
The New Serenity

German Pavilion at the 17th International Architecture Exhibition
— La Biennale di Venezia

Many of the contributions and considerations in this publication evolved in discussion with experts participating in 2038.

Sorry Press thanks 2038 and the contributors for granting us the rights to publish this book.

2038 is a non-profit organization.

Published by Sorry Press, Munich

Editor
Lukas Kubina

Associate Editors
Olaf Grawert & Christopher Roth
(2038)

Creative Direction
Wiegand von Hartmann

Design
Sophie von Hartmann,
Moritz Wiegand, Mohamad Fawal

Production
Eberl & Koesel

Cover Image
Gabriel von Max, *Affe vor Skelett*
(1900)

Printed in Germany
ISBN 978-3-9820440-4-0